the less-dead

the
less-dead

april lurie

delacorte press

All rights reserved. Published in the United States by Delacorte Press,
an imprint of Random House Children's Books,
a division of Random House, Inc., New York.

Delacorte Press is a registered trademark and the colophon is a
trademark of Random House, Inc.

Visit us on the Web! www.randomhouse.com/teens

Educators and librarians, for a variety of teaching tools, visit us at
www.randomhouse.com/teachers

Library of Congress Cataloging-in-Publication Data
Lurie, April.
The less-dead / April Lurie. — 1st ed.
p. cm.
Summary: Sixteen-year-old Noah Nordstrom, whose father is the host of a
popular evangelical Christian radio program, believes that the person who has
been killing gay teenagers in the Austin, Texas, foster care system is a regular
caller on his dad's show.
ISBN 978-0-385-73675-6 (hc : alk. paper) — ISBN 978-0-385-90626-5 (glb :
alk. paper) — ISBN : 978-0-375-89589-0 (e-book) [1. Murder—Fiction.
2. Homosexuality—Fiction. 3. Christian life—Fiction. 4. Conduct of life—
Fiction. 5. Austin (Tex.) 6. Mystery and detective stories.] I. Title.
PZ7.L97916Le 2010
[Fic]—dc22
2009018127

The text of this book is set in 12-point Goudy.

Book design by Kenny Holcomb

Printed in the United States of America

10 9 8 7 6 5 4 3 2 1

First Edition

For my husband, Ed,
who appreciates my dark side.
With love.

the less-dead

{prologue}

I find Will facedown in the woods near Barton Creek. For a split second I think he's asleep, or hurt, yeah, maybe just hurt. Will's crazy like that, camping out alone with no tent, not telling anyone where he is. But I realize it's wishful thinking; his body is splayed out in that sickening way you see on episodes of CSI.

My head starts to reel, so I grab what's closest—the trunk of a river birch—and hang on. I don't believe in signs or prophecies or visions from God, but Will's been missing twenty-four hours now, and when a dream woke me in the middle of the night, I knew he'd be here. In this exact spot.

I manage a few steps. In the distance, water surges over the rocks. Above, cicadas whir in the treetops. It's deafening. I kneel down. "Will? Hey, Will?" Crazy me, talking to a corpse.

I turn him over and see the bruises first—dark purple bands across his neck. Strangled, like the others. A circle of blood has soaked through his Kinks T-shirt, the one that used to belong to me. Will told me he liked the band, so I gave it to him. He said as payment he'd help me write a song for Aubrey, the girl who broke my heart right when all these crazy things started happening.

A corner of white catches my eye. Beside Will's head lies a small sheet of paper held in place by a limestone rock. The killer's note. I lift the rock and see letters cut from newspaper pasted to the page.

They parade their sin like Sodom;
They do not hide it. Woe to them!
Isaiah 3:9

I drop the rock. Beside the note is a coiled rope. The murder weapon.

I stare at the circle of blood fanning out from the center of Will's chest. Slowly, I lift his shirt, inching it up, little by little. My hands are shaking. There it is. A simple cross. A delicate, meticulous carving. The wound is raw, pink, glistening in the morning sun.

Cold sweat pours out of me. Blood sings in my ears. Before I know it, I'm puking my guts out. When I can finally stand, I reach for my cell phone, and that's when I see Will's small leather notebook of handwritten poems tossed aside in a pile of dead leaves. I pick it up and shove it into my back pocket. The police don't deserve his words. No one does, really. Then I dial 911.

{one}

I SUPPOSE my biggest problem is that my father is the Bible Answer Guy. In case you've never heard his radio show, it's on Monday through Friday, ten a.m., on KMBJ. Not that you'd actually *want* to tune in. You don't. First they play this seriously crappy inspirational music, and then my dad comes on to answer questions from listeners who call in from all over the country. He's pretty famous. But if you were feeling slightly masochistic and happened to check it out, it would give you a good idea of what it's like to be me—his sixteen-year-old son who despises church and religion and phony youth pastors who think it's their job to save your soul.

A highly popular question on my dad's program is "Dr. Nordstrom, what, in your opinion, is the unpardonable sin?" Well, I don't need my dad to answer that one. In my family, the unpardonable sin is getting sent to the Rock—an alternative school for juvenile delinquents—for eating Ritz crackers topped with apricot-hash jelly right before AP music theory. Which is what Carson, my best friend and fellow band member, and I did about a month ago.

It was early September, and technically, we were performing an experiment—to see how altered states of consciousness affected perceptions of tone and pitch. Very important if you aspire to play live music. We thought our teacher, Mr. Flynn, would be cool with this, since he's only twenty-five and supposedly open-minded, but we were wrong. And stupid. When he asked us to step outside class and tell him what was so hilarious about a G note on the treble clef, we told him about the jelly. Carson's recipe, by the way. He nodded and sighed and told us sadly that if he didn't report us, his job would be on the line. So he led Carson and me, like lambs to the slaughter, to the eleventh-grade principal, who sentenced us to sixty days.

As you can imagine, this whole ordeal was a complete embarrassment to my father. It's not easy to be the Bible Answer Guy when you've got a reprobate son. And since I'd been getting into quite a bit of trouble over the summer—making out in the woods with Aubrey at the You're Worth the Wait youth retreat, coming home drunk at four a.m. after a gig at Ben Huber's birthday party, and skipping church to get high with Carson at the Barton Creek Greenbelt—my parents decided to crack down on me, practice what they call tough love—a phrase coined by the Reverend Billy Graham or some other evangelical hotshot. Basically it means unlimited slave labor, a twelve o'clock curfew, and the removal of all evil influences from my life, Carson being number one on the list.

Obviously I didn't cooperate, and when my parents

realized I was a lost cause, they started locking me out of the house at night if I missed my curfew. But as it turned out, this punishment was harder on them than on me. I know this because my little sister, Melanie, always tells me about how Dad gets real quiet and Mom bawls her eyes out whenever I don't come home. Which makes me feel kind of guilty, but then again, I'm not the one turning the key, am I?

Anyway, I missed my curfew again, so that's why I'm standing here now at two in the morning, tossing pebbles at Carson's bedroom window. Finally it slides open, and his head pops out. "Noah? Is that you?" Carson's trying to grow dreadlocks, mostly to torture his dad, and right now he's got his hair tied up in a million multicolored rubber bands that are supposed to speed up the matting process. He looks like the Kosmic Koosh Ball I bought Melanie for Christmas last year.

"No, my sweet Roxanne," I say, "it is I, your beloved Cyrano."

He groans. "Noah, come on, give it up already."

"My nose may be large," I declare, "but other parts of me are even larger. Come into the light so I may gaze upon your beauty while I recite my love poems." This is sort of a running joke between me and Carson. After our English class read *Cyrano de Bergerac*, Carson started calling me Cyrano. Not because I have a huge schnoz or anything, but because I like poetry. So whenever I show up at Carson's window after midnight, I create a new balcony scene.

"Listen, I'll be right there. But keep your voice down. The DPCP just went to bed and he's *pissed*."

"Oh, okay. Sorry, man." DPCP stands for Demon-

Possessed Capitalist Pig. It's what Carson calls his father, who's the president of this very successful company that makes prosthetic limbs. You know, fake arms and legs. He's also an atheist, which I find rather fascinating.

I head to the backyard, and a minute later Carson unlocks the door of his 2.3-million-dollar house, located in one of the richest neighborhoods in Austin. Earlier tonight we played a gig at Greg Ziegler's party, and I was the only loser who had a curfew. Carson's parents are pretty strict, but not completely unreasonable like mine. "What happened?" he says. "You left the party at eleven. Said you'd make it home before twelve."

"Yeah, well, I got sidetracked."

"You mean you stopped by Aubrey's again. You're pathetic, Noah, you know that? Come on." He leads me into the kitchen, opens the freezer, and grabs two pints of Ben & Jerry's Cherry Garcia. I practically live at Carson's house and his mom buys it especially for me. "Let me guess," he says. "Aubrey's dad answered the door, whipped out a King James and a chastity belt, and preached to you about the evils of premarital sex."

Carson's trying to cheer me up, but I can barely crack a smile. Aubrey's father is the pastor of my church—a huge obstacle when it comes to my love life. "No. Aubrey answered the door, but she wouldn't let me in. Plus, she smelled *alcohol* on my breath, and *freaked*. Anyway, we got into a pretty bad argument. She . . . well, she said she didn't want to see me anymore."

Carson sighs and slides a pint of ice cream over to me. "Dig in, dude. It'll ease the pain."

I try a spoonful, but it doesn't work. The truth is I can't stop thinking about Aubrey. And even though Carson won't admit it, I know he misses her too. The three of us had been close friends since seventh grade, but everything got screwed up this summer at that stupid You're Worth the Wait youth retreat. Carson didn't go—the DPCP would never pay for a weekend of Christian propaganda—but Aubrey and I went, mostly because our parents twisted our arms, but we figured that between sessions on sexual purity, we could go water-skiing, blobbing, and zip-lining. We could also sneak out of class, which we did. One afternoon, Aubrey and I ditched "The Perils of Kissing," and after we laughed our heads off about it, Aubrey dared me to kiss her.

We were in the woods, halfway to the lake. At first I thought she was joking, but when I looked into her eyes, I saw that she wasn't. I'd been secretly lusting after Aubrey since the beginning of sophomore year, but we'd been friends so long I'd been afraid to make a move. Soon we were pressed up against a tree, making out like crazy, until a guy from Christian dork patrol spotted us. Aubrey got into a lot of trouble—her parents grounded her for two weeks—and when Carson and I got kicked out of school a few weeks later for the hash jelly experiment, Aubrey's father, Pastor Simpson, decided I was Satan's spawn and put his foot down. Outside church, Aubrey wasn't allowed to see me. Now I'd do anything to go back to the way things were. Even if it meant just being friends.

I take another spoonful of ice cream. "So, what's the DPCP pissed about this time?" I say.

Carson rolls his eyes. "Same old crap. He wants me to

get a job after school. Says I'm lazy and undisciplined." He screws up his face, pulls his dreads to the side like a comb-over, and does his best DPCP impersonation. "You'd better practice flipping burgers, Son, because the only people who'd hire you with that . . . that *hair* are the *freaks* at Lou's Grease Pit."

Carson's got me laughing now. I guess I'm lucky in a way. The Bible Answer Guy doesn't pressure me to get a job, because he's hoping I'll go back to pitching for McCallum High once I get out of the Rock. That's his other religion, by the way. Baseball.

"Or, how about this?" I say. "You could dress up like a slice of pizza and wave to people outside Hungry Howie's. That way, no one would see your hair *or* your face."

Carson glares at me. "Noah, come on, this is *not* funny! We're musicians! Artists! We can't be tied down to menial jobs. Besides, if you and I are ever going to write that break-out song—one that will rock the world—it's going to take time, sacrifice."

"True." I dig up a monster-sized cherry, pop it into my mouth, and chew. The taste reminds me of kissing Aubrey.

Carson's really wired now. He stands up and practically knocks over his chair. "Listen, Noah, we need to stop messing around. I mean, what are we doing playing gigs at high school parties? We're *way* too talented for that. Think about it! We live in *Austin*. The live-music capital of the world! We need to escape the evils of suburbia and get out there. Downtown! Sixth Street! The Drag!"

"But we're only sixteen," I say. "And we don't have any experience."

"It doesn't matter! Here, look at this." Carson grabs the entertainment section of the newspaper and points to a photo of a guy playing guitar. He has a mop of curly hair. "That's Sean Espinoza. He's *fifteen*. He plays Tuesdays at the Saxon Pub."

"Really?" I peer more closely. This guy Sean's got a real baby face. Pimples, too. I scan the article. It says that besides talent, Sean's got a solid work ethic, and if he keeps playing, he might be Austin's next Stevie Ray. "But I don't get it," I say. "I thought you had to be twenty-one to get into the Saxon Pub."

Carson groans like I'm the most naive guy on the planet, which I sort of am after having spent half my life in church. "Dude, not if you're the *performing artist*. Look, right here it says that Sean began as a street performer on the Drag. People liked his music, word got around, and next thing you know, he's a star! Come on, what do you say we go down there tomorrow?"

"Hmmm . . ." I don't have the heart to tell Carson that tomorrow, Saturday, to atone for my many sins, I'm supposed to cut the grass, weed-whack, and paint the back fence. But suddenly an idea pops into my head. The Drag, aka Guadalupe Street, is where the zealots from my youth group go every Saturday to witness to the lost. They claim Satan has a stronghold on the Drag because of its new age shops, tattoo parlors, dive bars, and drug dealers, and they have to win it back for the Lord. Anyway, my parents would never refuse if I told them I wanted to hang with the youth group on Saturday. And if I was bringing Carson along, well, maybe he'd listen to the gospel and get saved. Of course, little would they know, Carson and I would be spreading our own gospel: rock and roll.

"What do you say, Noah? Are you with me or not?"

"Yeah, man. I'm with you. Totally."

"All right, then." Carson holds out his fist. I bump it. "Tomorrow, we take our guitars to the Drag. Show Austin what we've got."

We finish off the pints of Ben & Jerry's, and Carson heads back to bed. I'm not tired yet, so I spread out the newspaper on the kitchen table. I'm about to reread the Sean Espinoza story, but something else catches my eye. A blurb on the front page of the Metro section.

SUSPECT ARRESTED IN
MURDER OF GAY TEEN

A man is being held without bail for the brutal murder of Austin teenager Kyle Lester, who was found dead on Sept. 9 in the back alley of Urban Legend, a popular gay bar on Sixth Street—the city's live-entertainment district.

I can hardly breathe. About a month ago, right before I got kicked out of school and things were getting pretty hairy between me and my parents, there was this psycho who kept calling in to my dad's radio show. The guy seemed intelligent and knowledgeable about the Bible, but after a while it was clear that he was completely warped. He'd call in with a question but would soon begin to rant about Austin's gay community and how God was going to bring judgment upon them.

My dad always gave the guy his lame, standard answer concerning homosexuality—hate the sin but love the sinner—but soon the guy became so angry and belligerent that my father stopped taking his calls. One week later, a gay eighteen-year-old boy, Kyle Lester, was strangled to death outside Urban Legend. A cross had been carved into his chest. The killer left behind a rope, the murder weapon. Along with it, a note—letters cut from newspaper.

Leviticus 18:22
Thou shALt Not LIe wIth
MANKINd, As wIth wOMANKINd:
It Is ABOMINAtIon.

{two}

SATURDAY MORNING, I jog home from Carson's, sneak past my parents, who are drinking coffee on the back patio, and tiptoe into Melanie's room. I swear, the kid is such a sack rat. It's eleven o'clock and she's still sound asleep. I take a seat on her bed, pleased to see the collection of poetry I gave her for her ninth birthday this year sitting on the night table. Since the only books in our family's library are Bibles, Bible commentaries, and inspirational junk about how to live an exciting Christian life (oxymoron, if you ask me), I figure someone has to enlighten her.

I open to the page she's dog-eared—"Stopping by Woods on a Snowy Evening," by Robert Frost—and run my finger across the first three lines she's underlined all wiggly in pencil.

The woods are lovely, dark and deep,
But I have promises to keep,
And miles to go before I sleep,

"Noah?" She smiles dreamily and is about to reach out and give me hug, but then she sticks out her tongue and rolls over. "You're a big fat liar! Go away!"

"Hey, come on, Mel. All right, so I didn't come home last night. So I'm not perfect. But, listen, there's a reason."

She throws a stuffed lizard at me; its beady eye scrapes my cheek. "Yeah, like *what?*"

"Ouch! Jeez, Mel! I stopped by Aubrey's after our gig, all right?"

Melanie's quiet now and I can tell she's thinking things over. She misses Aubrey almost as much as I do. Before the whole mess happened, Aubrey used to hang out at our house all the time. She'd braid Melanie's hair, paint her toenails, give her advice about boys. Slowly, Melanie turns around. Her eyes are puffy, like she went to bed crying. I hope it wasn't because of me. "So . . . what did Aubrey say? Does she want to be friends again?"

"Well, it was late and she couldn't really talk, but I'm working on it, okay?"

Melanie sighs. Then she looks at me all serious and her chin begins to quiver. "Noah, I'm scared. I heard Mom and Dad talking last night. They said if you keep getting into trouble, they're going to send you away. To a farm or something, where they keep horses and pigs and chickens. I don't want you to go!"

"Oh, come on, Mel. No one's sending me anywhere. Besides, I'd never leave you." I make a goofy face and tickle her; she starts to laugh. My parents think they're hiding something, but I've seen the stuff that's been coming in the mail lately—pamphlets about Christian farms for troubled youths. The idea is that if you pay a butt-load of money, your delinquent kid gets his very own horse to care for. Which sounds pretty cool, right? But here's the catch. The farms are like fascist right-wing military schools. No phones, no radio, no secular music, no coed mingling, and the only book you can read is the Bible. Screw that.

I hear footsteps in the hallway. I can tell it's my dad, because he's got these brand-new tennis shoes that squeak. Melanie's door is slightly ajar and he raps it a few times. "Noah, is that you?"

"Oh, come in, Daddy," Melanie says. "Noah's here and he's *absolutely* fine. The reason he was late last night is because he went to visit Aubrey. So, he's not in trouble, right?"

When my dad enters, I study his face, wondering if he's seen the article in the paper about the murder suspect. It's hard to tell. I brace myself for a proverb like *As a dog returns to its vomit, so a fool repeats his folly*, but instead, he just sighs and pats Melanie on the head. He looks worn out, which may not be a bad thing for me. "Well, sweetie, I'm glad Noah's home, and I'm glad he's fine, but—"

Before he can go any further, I say, "Dad, I'm *really* sorry about last night. What happened was, I stopped by Aubrey's after our gig and I didn't realize how late it got." I take a deep breath and try to look as sincere as possible. "I know I have a lot of work to do around the house, but, well, I was wondering if I could go to the Drag today. You know, with the youth group? Carson wants to go too. I'll cut the grass and weed-whack and paint the fence and do whatever else you want tomorrow, okay? After church."

The "after church" insert was brilliant, if I do say so

myself. Also, notice I didn't lie. I never said Carson and I would be *witnessing* on the Drag. It's one of those sins of omission, which, in my opinion, is about on the same level as coveting your neighbor's ox or donkey.

My plan seems to be working. I've definitely thrown my father off guard (his jaw is hanging open) and Melanie's helping me out by making these big, sad pleading eyes. "Well, I suppose you could do your chores tomorrow," he says. "But I'm a little confused, Noah. Why the sudden change of heart? And now *Carson* wants to join you? It's all very odd, to say the least."

This is true. My father might be a sucker when it comes to wanting to save my soul, but he's no dope. He graduated with honors from UT Law School and went on to Dallas Theological Seminary, where he became an expert on eschatology or whatever you call that end-time crap. As he stands there tapping his foot and waiting for my explanation, my mom walks in. Perfect timing. "Noah! Oh, thank goodness you're home." She breathes a sigh of relief and gives my father a scolding look. "John, why didn't you tell me?"

"Oh, sorry, hon, I was about to, I just . . ." FYI: my mother is the only person who can render the Bible Answer Guy speechless.

She walks over and gives me a hug, then pulls away all hurt and disappointed, which kind of kills me. "We were *very* worried about you, Noah." I can tell she's about to ask where I stayed last night but stops herself. It's all part of the tough love thing. Pretty ridiculous, if you ask me.

"I know. I'm sorry, Mom. I won't let it happen again. I promise."

My dad clears his throat. "Laura, Noah's asking to go to the Drag today with the youth group. What do you think? Can he do his chores tomorrow?"

Her eyes widen. "The youth group? Why . . . sure. Of course. Um, that's wonderful." I haven't shown interest in attending youth group meetings since eighth grade, so this is probably quite a shock to her. Fortunately my mom doesn't question my motives. Now I need to get out of the house as quickly as possible.

"Okay, well, great," I say. "I better hit the shower and get a move on." I tickle Melanie in the ribs one last time. "See you later, kid."

I shower, get dressed, and grab my guitar and harmonicas, and just as I'm about to walk out the door, I see my dad sitting in his study, staring at the wall. It's risky to go in there now—he may have caught on to my devious scheme—but I do anyway. "Dad?" He turns to me. His eyes are a little glassy. "Um, did you see the article in the paper yesterday? You know, about the murder?"

He nods. "Yes, I did."

"Looks like they caught the guy, huh?"

He sighs deeply. "I hope so, Noah. I really do." Right after we heard the news that Kyle Lester had been killed, my father contacted the police. The murder was a pretty high-profile case in Austin, probably because the city, smack in the middle of the Bible Belt, is an oasis for gays and lesbians. It was a long shot that the psycho calling in to my dad's radio show was the killer, but still, the cops followed up on every possible lead. The investigation went nowhere. The guy was like a ghost.

"Yeah, me too," I say. "So have the police called you? Do you know who they arrested? It didn't say much in the paper."

"No. I don't know anything. I'm not sure I want to either." There's a moment of awkward silence, and then my dad says, "Well, have a good time today. I'll put some gas in the Weedwacker so you'll be all set for tomorrow."

"Oh, okay, thanks, Dad." What I really want to do is tell my father I'm sorry for what I said that night, one week after Kyle's murder, when I came home drunk from Ben Huber's party. When my father saw that I'd been drinking, he started going off on me about how I'd turned my back on my family, on my church, and, worst of all, on God.

I couldn't take it anymore. "Turned my back on *God?*" I screamed. "You're *such* a hypocrite! Just like all the other phonies at church. You think you're better than everyone else because you're a Christian? All you do is spread *hate* on your stupid radio show. You say, 'Hate the sin, but love the sinner'? Well, let me ask you something, Dad. How are you supposed to love a gay person when you've never even *known* one? You pass judgment on people, condemn them for who they are. You could have done the right thing, stood up to that caller, but you didn't. The truth is, *you're* the one responsible for Kyle Lester's murder. That's right, *you!* The Bible Answer Guy."

He raised a hand like he was going to hit me, and honestly, I wouldn't have blamed him if he had. It was a rotten thing to say. Besides, who was I to talk? Sure, I knew some gay kids at school, but it wasn't like I was friends with any of them. Did I even want to be?

My father's hand fell to his side. He started to cry. I stood there, stunned. My father's not an emotional person, and I'd never seen him cry before. But there was no way to make this right, so I walked away, slammed my bedroom door behind me. For once, he was the person being judged.

To my surprise, in the morning, my father skipped the lecture, reached out, and gave me a hug. I had a wicked hangover—my head was splitting, and my stomach churning—but I managed to hug him back. "What's past is past," he said. "Let's move on."

But I don't know. Words like mine are not easily forgiven.

Or forgotten.

{three}

CARSON AND I set up on the corner of Twenty-third and Guadalupe and begin our Austin debut with a little Pearl Jam. After that, it's Smashing Pumpkins, and soon we're rocking out on Jet's "Are You Gonna Be My Girl." Our plan was to start out with a few cover songs to draw people in, and it's working. A small crowd of UT students is gathered around, seriously digging our music, and dollar bills are piling up in our guitar cases. One guy throws in a five. I'm beginning to wonder if Carson and I can make a living doing this.

Across Guadalupe, on the sidewalk of the UT campus, the Christian youth group zealots are handing out cartoon tracts entitled *Heaven or Hell: Which Will You Choose?* I've seen the tracts before. On page one, St. Peter is welcoming this repentant drug addict into the pearly gates, but on page two, there's good old Lucifer, complete with horns and pointy tail, tossing some poor sucker—a college professor holding a book by Friedrich Nietzsche with the slogan "God Is Dead"—into the lake of fire. A pretty obvious scare tactic, if you ask me.

Anyway, when we first arrived, to keep up appearances *and* stay out of trouble, I checked in with Marty, our twenty-three-year-old youth pastor, who thinks he's all hip and cool, all down with the teen scene, which he's *not*. Then I stuffed some tracts into my pocket and told him I'd be performing music across the street with Carson. I guess he assumed we'd be playing upbeat Christian songs, but what he doesn't know won't hurt him, right? I'm so pumped up right now from doing Jet's song that I want to scream, *Hell! I choose hell, you idiots!* but then I see Carson pointing across the street. "Whoa, look at that!"

A skater dude, about our age, is carrying a big wooden ramp over his head. Marty helps him set the ramp in the street and begins placing orange cones around it to ward off cars. Next the skater picks up his board and starts doing all these amazing stunts. Meanwhile our fans are crossing Guadalupe to watch, and the youth group is having a field day handing out their tracts.

"Who *is* that guy?" I say, mostly to myself. "I've never seen him at church before."

"Hmmm, I don't know," Carson says. "But isn't that Aubrey?"

"Huh?" Aubrey has always been anti–street evangelism. Like me, she believes that if a person wants to find God, God will find him or her. But there she is, looking especially beautiful, leaning against the UT campus wall and watching the skater. Standing next to her is a girl I don't recognize.

Carson's mouth hangs open. "Wait a minute, who's the girl with Aubrey?" His eyes are glazing over, and he's got that hungry, horny wolf look. "Noah, come on, grab your stuff. Let's go over there and say hi."

One thing about Carson is that he has no idea when a girl is completely out of his league. Which is most of the time, including right now. The girl standing next to Aubrey is *hot*. "I don't know, man. I don't think it's a good idea—"

But before I can object any further, Carson's packing up our guitar cases and pulling me across the street. "Hey, Aubrey!" he shouts.

When Aubrey sees me, she frowns and folds her arms across her chest. I wonder if *she's* seen the article in the paper about the murder suspect. I know she'd be interested. Suddenly I'm desperate to talk to her about it. Aubrey was always the one I could confide in, but not anymore. Carson sets down the cases, smiles at the new girl, and holds out one hand. "Hi, I'm Carson, and this is Noah. Don't believe *anything* Aubrey's told you about us."

The girl laughs and shakes his hand. Carson holds on to it longer than he needs to. "All right," she says. "I won't. I'm Kat. I just moved here from Dallas. Are you guys with King of Glory?"

King of Glory Christian Center is the name of our church. Well, my *parents'* church. Except for a grueling hour on Sunday mornings, I try to avoid the place as much as possible. Which is difficult, since Aubrey's father is the founding pastor. Carson's been there a couple of times with me, mostly to piss off his dad, but he's certainly no regular. Too hard-core for a guy who's been told all his life that religion is the opium of the masses. "Oh, *yeah*," he says. "Yeah, we go there."

Aubrey rolls her eyes. "What are you guys doing here, anyway?"

"What do you mean?" Carson says, looking all offended. "We're here to spread the Word."

"Spread the *Word?*" I say. I expect Carson to break into his highly entertaining impersonation of a televangelist, but he doesn't.

"Yes." He shoots me a warning look and turns to Kat. "Noah and I were just playing some gospel music across the street, and now"—he digs into his pocket and pulls out a tract—"we're going to witness to the lost."

Kat seems to think Carson is incredibly funny. She's also buying his story. "Great, that's what we were about to do," she says.

I raise an eyebrow at Aubrey. She looks away. I inch closer to her and whisper, "Did you see the article in the paper? About the murder? They caught the guy, the one who killed Kyle Lester."

She looks at me, stunned. "Wow, that's great. I'm glad they finally got him." For the moment, she doesn't seem angry with me anymore. It's almost like we're back to being friends. She's about to say something else, but now the skater dude comes flying toward us.

"Hey, girls, what's up?" He's wearing a T-shirt that says *Got Jesus?* In fact, he kind of looks like Jesus: long hair, carpenter's build, life-of-the-party kind of guy. He hops backward off his board and uses just enough upward torque to catch it with one hand. "Hey," he says, "you're Noah, right? Son of the famous Bible Answer Guy?"

"Uh . . . yeah." I don't like the way this guy is standing so close to Aubrey. Like he owns her or something. Also, how does he know my name? Probably heard it from Marty, who no doubt clued him in that I was a pagan.

"Cool," he says. "I'm Brandon. I guess you already met my sister, Kat. Anyway, I'm a big fan of your father's. I tune in to his show whenever I can."

"Groovy," I say, although I doubt he catches my sarcasm. Actually, I'm barely listening to this guy. Mostly I'm watching the way his arm is brushing against Aubrey's and how she doesn't seem to mind it one bit.

"Hey, I like your dreads," he says to Carson. "I tried to grow those once, but, well, let's just say it didn't work out."

Carson beams and touches his nasty locks. "Thanks. The trick is the rubber bands."

"Brandon, this is Carson," Kat says. "He goes to King of Glory."

"Awesome." Brandon slips his hand into Aubrey's. My stomach plummets. "So are you guys here to evangelize and hand out tracts too?" he says.

"No," I answer, staring hard at Aubrey.

"Oh, *I* am," Carson says. "But, well, I'm sort of new at it, so maybe"—he grins at Kat—"I could tag along with you?"

"Sure," she says.

I glare at Carson; he ignores me.

"We'll do guy-girl teams," Brandon says. "That's how

Marty likes it." He looks at me. "You, uh, sure you don't want to join us, Noah? We could use your expertise."

Expertise? Is this guy kidding? "Yeah, I'm sure. Actually, I was planning to wander around, check out the new age shops, buy some tarot cards, score a gram or two."

"Oh, okay," Brandon says, laughing. "I guess we'll hook up with you later."

God, this guy is such an idiot. "Yeah, later." I pick up both guitar cases and whisper to Carson, "See you around, *Judas*."

{four}

NOW THAT Carson's been born again, I guess I have to go solo. I walk several yards to the UT campus's main entrance, take out my guitar, strap on my funky harmonica headgear, and find a seat on the concrete steps. I'm in a pretty melancholy mood right now, so I decide to sing some haunting old folk tunes by Lead Belly.

It's kind of weird—most people think I don't believe in God, but I do. I pray when I'm alone, and it's like me and God are having a conversation, even though I do the talking. It was a couple of years ago, right around the time I discovered what my dad would call worldly pleasures—art, poetry, literature, and secular music—that I realized how much I was missing. I figured out that I don't need a church or a sermon or a plan of salvation to feel close to God. All I need is my music.

I begin with "Where Did You Sleep Last Night?" Mr. Flynn, our former AP music theory teacher, was the one who introduced us to Lead Belly. And even though Mr. Flynn ultimately hung me and Carson out to dry for the hash jelly experiment, I have to thank him for opening my mind to new genres. After I heard Lead Belly, something inside me changed and I began to think about my music in a totally different way.

I sing the chorus a few times: *"My girl, my girl, don't lie to me. Tell me where did you sleep last night?"* Then I close my eyes and play the melody on the harp. The notes are all minors and it almost sounds like my harmonica is crying.

"Man, someone must have seriously broken your heart."

I open my eyes and see this tall, wiry guy—about my age, maybe a little older—standing on the steps right in front of me. He's got pale blue eyes, and he's watching me intently. His hair's pale too—blond and long, reaching to his shoulders. There's something familiar about him, but I can't place him. "No, don't stop," he says. "Keep playing. It just sounds so sad, you know?"

"Okay." I shrug and continue. *"In the pines, in the pines, where the sun don't ever shine, I would shiver the whole night through . . ."* This time I keep my eyes open. I sing the chorus a few more times, and when I finish, he smiles. He's good-looking in that grungy, bohemian kind of way. No doubt he's had better luck with girls than I have.

"Hey, is it all right if I sit down?" he asks.

"Yeah, go ahead."

He pulls a small leather notebook and a pen from his back pocket, takes a seat beside me, and begins to write.

"Um, what are you doing?" I ask.

"Oh, I'm jotting down those lyrics, if that's okay. I've never heard that song before. It's great."

"Thanks. It's an old slave song, by a guy named Lead Belly."

He looks up. "Lead Belly?"

"Yeah. He was this real tough dude who supposedly had an iron gut for liquor. He played a twelve-string and sang gospel and blues. His music's amazing."

The guy nods. "Cool. I'll remember that. Thanks." He finishes writing, closes the book, and looks at me. "Anyway, was I right? Did someone just break your heart?"

I nod. "Yeah. Last night my girlfriend, well, ex-girlfriend, I guess—it's complicated—anyway, her name's Aubrey; she told me she didn't want to see me anymore."

"Rough."

"Yeah, she's over there with a skater named Brandon. Do you see him? The guy who looks like Jesus? They're witnessing to the lost souls on the Drag."

He peers across the street and smiles wryly. "Lost souls, huh? You mean like me?"

"Yeah," I say. "Like you and me."

He lifts his chin. "See Doomsday over there?"

Across the street, standing on the steps of the Methodist church, is the old, bearded homeless man, a street evangelist who's been a fixture on the Drag for as long as I can remember. Today he's wearing a sign that reads ARMAGEDDON IS NOW! "Yeah, I see him here all the time," I say. "Is that his name? Doomsday?"

"Yep. He's a friend of mine."

"Really?"

"Don't be shocked. Doomsday's an interesting guy once you get to know him. But when he's all riled up, he likes to preach at me, tell me how the end is near and how I need to get right with God. I always tell him the same thing: I *am* right with God. And I'm not afraid of dying."

Personally, I *am* afraid of dying, but I decide to keep it to myself. This whole conversation is pretty strange. I've known this guy for, what, five minutes and we've already discussed my nonexistent love life, God, and death. I'm not really sure what to do at this point, so I hold out my hand. "Hey, I'm Noah." We shake.

"Nice to meet you, Noah. I'm Will."

That's when I notice a tattoo on the inside of his right forearm. In black letters are the words "The Road Not Taken."

"Hey," I say. "That tattoo on your arm, it's—"

"A poem," he says. "Do you know it?"

"Of course," I say. "It's one of my favorites." In the same way Lead Belly changed how I thought about music, that poem by Robert Frost changed how I thought about words.

He stares at the tattoo and recites, "'Two roads diverged in a wood, and I . . .'" He waits for me to say the next line.

"'I took the one less traveled by.'"

He looks up. "'And that has made all the difference.'"

Suddenly I remember where I've seen Will. At school. "Hey, do you go to the Rock?"

"Ahhh, yeah." He leans back and studies me. "You've got a friend, right? With the funky hair?"

"Yeah, that's Carson." I point across the street, where

28

Kat is talking to a college student. Carson's standing right behind her, like he's an evangelist in training, but actually he's just staring at her ass. "Today we were supposed to be making our Austin music debut, but instead, he met a girl from church and got saved in two seconds flat."

"Oh, right, I see him," Will says. "Looks like his mind is really on the Lord, huh?" He laughs. "So, anyway, how'd you and Carson wind up at the Rock? You guys seem pretty harmless."

"Oh, we, uh, ate some hash jelly on crackers, right before music theory. It was sort of an experiment."

He grins. "An experiment? Now, *that's* original."

"Yeah, I suppose it is. So, how about you? Why are you there?"

"Oh, well . . ." He winces. "That's a long, tragic story. One you probably don't want to hear."

I shrug. "Try me. I've got plenty of time. Carson's in full evangelical mode. Aubrey's busy with *Brandon*. Looks like I'll be sitting here for a while doing nothing." I take off my harmonica headpiece and set it on my lap.

Will gives me a strange look, sighs deeply, and gazes up at the sky. "Why does this always happen with guitarists?"

"What?" I say. "What are you talking about?"

"Nothing. Forget it." He plucks the pen from behind his ear and taps it against his book a few times. "All right, fine, I'll tell you my tragic story. But I'll have to start from the beginning. Otherwise, you wouldn't understand. You'd just think I was a major asshole."

"I doubt it, but all right. Go ahead. Start from the beginning."

"Okay. You see, both my parents died when I was ten years old. Killed in a car wreck."

I sit there blinking. This is not what I was expecting at all. "Hey, listen, Will, I'm sorry, I didn't realize—"

Will holds up one hand. "Look, you don't have to feel bad. I mean, it was a long time ago. It sucks, but I'm used to it now. Anyway, I had no other family to take me in, so after my parents died, I became property of the state. Since then I've lived in a lot of places—group homes, shelters, foster care—and, well, this last foster home in Austin . . . let's just say I *really* had to get out. So I made the mistake of meeting with this dealer in town. He was selling high-quality weed— real expensive stuff. My idea was to work for him for a while, make a ton of money, and get out of here—head back to California, which is where I'm originally from. But it didn't work out. Turned out there were a couple of undercover cops working at Anderson High—that's where I used to go—and I got busted selling weed to some rich congressman's kid. The police kept the details a secret, sent me to the Rock, and cut me this deal where I'd get off pretty easy if I helped them out."

As I'm listening to Will's crazy story, I'm also thinking about Kyle Lester. After his murder, I scoured the newspapers, trying to find out as much about him as I could. But there wasn't much to know, except that he had no family and had been in foster care most of his life. Just like Will. When Kyle turned eighteen, he was out on the streets, and a few months later, he was killed. "Um, what do you mean?" I say. "How did you help the cops?"

Will studies me for a moment, leans in closer, and

whispers, "You see, there was this detective. He wanted me to wear a wire, so I did, and they caught the guy."

"But I don't understand," I say. "I mean, you're a kid in high school. That sounds really dangerous."

"Yeah, I guess. Maybe if I had a family, they would have thought twice about it, but I don't. And I know what you're thinking. That I'm a narc, right? Well, maybe I am, but the guy sitting in jail right now is a rotten bastard, so I really don't care."

I shake my head. "No. That's not what I was thinking. I just didn't know cops could do stuff like that. You know, *use* people our age."

He laughs and shrugs. "'I'm nobody! Who are you? Are you nobody, too?'"

"Emily Dickinson."

"Right. Come on, Noah, everyone gets used one way or another. Besides, I don't think the cops look at it that way. For them, they're just doing their job."

Across the street, Doomsday marches to the corner and begins delivering one of his hellfire-and-brimstone sermons. Will smiles and shakes his head. "Here we go again." But soon a young ponytailed guy, carrying a bedroll and walking a mangy-looking dog, strolls over to Doomsday and puts an arm around his shoulder. Doomsday shrugs him off and continues his rant.

The guy gives up. He cups a hand around his mouth and calls, "Will! Hey, come on, I need your help!"

"All right," Will calls back. "Humor him for a while. I'll be there soon."

"Is the guy with the dog a friend of yours too?" I say.

31

"Yep, that's Quindlan. He showed up on the Drag about six months ago. Since then he's been hanging out with Doomsday and me. The three of us are pretty close. Anyway, I better go. I'll look for you around school, okay? Maybe we can hang out?" Will stands, cocks his head to one side, and points to my T-shirt. "Cool shirt. The Kinks are like my all-time favorite band. Do you and Carson cover them?"

"Yeah." I pick up my guitar and play a few bars of "You Really Got Me."

Will grins. "You're really good. You know, you should write that girl Aubrey a song. Sad and sweet like the one you were playing before." He pats the notebook in his back pocket. "That's what I do. If I'm feeling down, or I need to get something out, I write poetry."

"That's cool, but . . ." I shake my head. "Nah, I've tried to write songs. They suck. I mean, I can write the music okay, but the words are all wrong."

"Dude, don't give up. Sometimes I get stuck on words, but then I remember what Bob Dylan said. 'A poem is a naked person,' and 'A song is anything that can walk by itself.'"

"A poem is a naked person," I say. "Huh. I like that."

"Yeah, I do too."

"Hey, Will, before you go, there's something I want to ask you. I know it's a long shot, but did you by any chance know Kyle Lester? The guy who was murdered outside Urban Legend about a month ago? I remember reading in the paper that he'd been a foster kid."

Will nods sadly. "Actually, yeah, I knew Kyle. We weren't good friends or anything, but about a year ago we lived in the same group home. Why?"

"I'm not sure if you heard, but they arrested a suspect in his murder. I read it in the paper yesterday."

His eyes widen. "Really? That's great news. I'm glad they got that psycho off the streets. Hey, thanks for telling me."

I watch Will walk down the steps. He's about to cross the street, but then I get an idea. "Will, hold on!" He turns around.

I stand up, pull off my Kinks shirt, and toss it to him. "Keep it," I say.

He looks at me like I'm crazy. "What? No way!"

"Really, man, I want you to have it. Besides"—I stretch out my arms to the sky—"I need to practice what Bob Dylan said, right?"

He watches me for a while. I expect him to laugh, but he doesn't. He just stands there, staring. Across the street, Doomsday and Quindlan are staring at me too. Suddenly I feel very naked.

"All right," Will says. "I'll keep the shirt. But nothing's free. As payment, I'll help you write that song for Aubrey."

"Okay. Fair enough."

He waves goodbye, then walks across the Drag, dodging a taxi, and joins Doomsday and Quindlan.

A cool breeze blows. I've got goose bumps now. I cross my arms over my chest. The next thing I know, Carson is climbing the steps toward me. "Noah? What are you doing? Seriously, dude, I know you've got a decent build and everything, but there *are* other ways of getting Aubrey's attention."

{five}

"SO TELL me the truth, Noah. These church girls, is it really true that they won't put out until they're, like, married?"

It's Monday morning, and Carson and I have just passed through the metal detectors at the Rock. Carson came with me to church yesterday, and when Kat invited him to the movies this Friday night with the youth group, he immediately thought she was into him. Since then, he's been scheming ways to get her alone and, hopefully, get into her pants.

We pause for a moment, turn our empty pockets inside out to show the security guards that we're not planning to stab ourselves or anyone else with a pen in the bathroom today, and continue down the hallway. "Carson, shut up, all right? I'm sick of hearing about this. Besides, is that all you care about? Getting laid?"

"Well, no. It's not *all* I care about. But it *is* a concern. I'm sixteen. A junior. The bases are loaded, dude. I'd like to at least *think* I'm on my way to scoring a home run."

Carson's bases are far from loaded, but I decide not to mention it. And while it's true that we're both hoping to lose our virginity in the not-too-distant future, *I* at least have a few standards. Like being in love. Which sounds pretty corny, I know, but after kissing Aubrey, the thought of *doing it* with someone else doesn't seem right. "Yeah, well, the answer is yes. They don't put out. So just keep on *thinking*."

The nasty odor of pork and beans is already wafting from the cafeteria. That's another perk of being a student at the Rock. We're served the same no-frills menu as the hard-core criminals at juvie. And forget about packing a lunch, since you never know—there might be vodka mixed in with our OJ, or weed baked into our brownies.

"Hey, isn't that Will over there by the lockers?" Carson says.

I take a look. Sure enough, it is. "Yeah, that's him." Over the weekend I told Carson all about Will—how he lost his family, how he's had to live in group homes and foster care, how he got busted for dealing and wound up wearing a wire for the police.

"Look at that. He's wearing your Kinks shirt."

As Will pops open his locker, Hawk—a loner goth with a spiked Mohawk and a silver bolt through his nose—comes up behind him. I don't know the dude's real name; I'm not sure anyone does. Mostly, he roams the halls like a ghost. He pats Will on the back; Will turns around and they greet each other.

"They're friends, you know," Carson says. "Hawk and Will. I've seen them together."

"Really?" This strikes me as odd. I didn't think Hawk had any friends at school.

Suddenly Will sees us. "Hey, Noah! Carson! Come on over."

"Oh, great," Carson says. "Let's hope the security guards aren't watching us. The other day I saw Hawk buying dope from Justin Kingsley."

"Come on, don't be so paranoid," I say, although Carson has a legitimate point. At the Rock, guilt by association can be lethal.

Hawk studies me carefully as we walk toward the lockers. His Mohawk is dyed bloodred today, and he's wearing heavy black eyeliner. I've never seen the guy smile, but strangely one side of his mouth is curled up.

Will says hi and introduces us to Hawk, who nods solemnly. Then Will holds out a fist to Carson. "I hear you're pretty good on guitar too," he says.

Carson shrugs and taps Will's fist. "I'm all right. Noah's better."

This is true, but Carson likes to play up his false humility. It can be pretty irritating.

Meanwhile Hawk is looking me up and down, and it's making me uncomfortable. "So, you're Noah," he says. "The guitarist from the Drag. The one who likes poetry. Will told me about you."

"Oh yeah?" I say, stunned by the number of words Hawk just uttered. "Good things, I hope?"

But before Hawk can answer, three policemen turn the corner. They march directly toward us.

"Shit," Hawk says. "Here they come."

The officers surround Hawk. One starts reciting, "You

have the right to remain silent. Anything you say can and will be used against you in a court of law. . . ."

"Spare me," Hawk says, rolling his eyes. He holds out both wrists to the second officer, who quickly slaps on a set of handcuffs.

I look at Carson. His jaw is hanging open. We've seen arrests at the Rock before, but none this close.

"Move away now, boys," the third officer says to us.

But Will doesn't listen. He steps right up to Hawk. "Hey, are you going to be all right?"

"I'll be fine," Hawk says. "But what about you?"

"Don't worry about me."

"Move away," the police officer repeats.

Will steps back. The cops shuffle Hawk past us. As they do, Hawk gives me a pleading look and whispers, "Noah, do me a favor, all right? Take care of Will."

I nod and watch while the cops march him down the hall. The late bell rings. The security guard bellows, "Get to class! Now!"

† † †

"I want everyone to close their eyes, and listen to a poem by William Carlos Williams, entitled 'The Red Wheelbarrow.'" It's been several hours since we saw Hawk get arrested, and I've spent most of the morning shaking it off. Now I'm sitting in English, my last class of the day, and Mr. Dobbs is reading us poetry. One very surprising thing about the Rock is that the teachers are pretty cool. And it's not like they got fired from their old jobs and had to take sucky positions teaching juvenile delinquents; they're here because they *want* to be. Some even have PhDs, like Mr. Dobbs, who used to be a professor at UT. Once, he told our class that he wanted to make an impact on kids at risk. He said it gave his life meaning.

Anyway, last week we read selections from the legendary rapper Tupac Shakur's *The Rose That Grew from Concrete*. The poems were kind of depressing, but very well done, and the whole thing went over *really* big in class, since there are a lot of gangster types here at the Rock, and Tupac is their *god*. Even the major badasses were totally into it.

I'm pretty excited, because this week we're beginning a new section on the imagists. I've read "The Red Wheelbarrow" before. I have a collection by Williams at home, but for some reason his poems really come alive when Mr. Dobbs reads them aloud.

I close my eyes. He recites, "'So much depends upon—a red wheelbarrow—glazed with rainwater—beside the white chickens.'" He pauses a moment. "The poem paints a picture. Do you see it?"

Yeah, I do. I open my eyes and see all the badasses nodding in agreement. "Besides being a poet, Williams was also a medical doctor," Mr. Dobbs explains. "This poem is said to be a depiction of what he saw while tending to a very sick girl in her home."

I'm not sure why, but knowing this gives me a lump in my throat. It makes me admire Williams's work even more.

"And now," Mr. Dobbs says, "I'd like you to write your own poems using this model. I want you to begin with the words 'So much depends upon.'" He passes out paper and pencils, and no one even complains. "Remember, use an image. Make it vivid. Your words should create a snapshot in time."

We start, and as usual I have no idea what to write. I try "So much depends upon my guitar," but that turns out lame, so I decide to be romantic and write, "So much depends upon a girl," but the words are sappy and sentimental. I sigh and turn my paper over. I write, "So much depends upon the murder of Kyle Lester." But I don't know where to go from there, seeing that Kyle Lester's dead, and no poem, no matter how good it is, is going to bring him back.

"Are you having trouble, Noah?" Mr. Dobbs says.

"Yeah, I guess I am."

"Well, maybe I can spark an idea." He shuffles through some papers, and when he finds the one he's looking for, he holds it up and smiles. "Class, I'd like you to take a break for a moment and listen to a poem written by a student in second period. Again, I want you to close your eyes, and picture the scene."

He clears his throat and begins.

"So much depends upon
a white boy,
singing a slave song on the dirty steps,
eyes closed, strumming steel,
a lost soul, like me."

My eyes pop open. Mr. Dobbs is looking right at me. "Noah? Are you okay?" he asks.

"Yeah," I say. "I'm fine."

{six}

"I DON'T get it. Why does so much depend upon *me?*"

I find Will sitting on a bench by the outdoor basketball courts. He looks up, startled. "Noah. Hey, I'm glad you found me. Oh." He lowers his eyes; his face reddens. "You read my poem?"

"Well, not exactly." I take a seat next to him. "Mr. Dobbs read it to our class. It was good—I mean, I liked it, but . . . why?"

He stares across the empty courts, chewing his bottom lip. He doesn't say anything for a while. That's when I notice that his clothes are filthy—smudged with soot. Bits of dried leaves are stuck to his shoelaces. He smells of smoke, like he's been sitting around a campfire. Strange, I must not have noticed it this morning. On the ground, beside Will's feet, lay two plastic grocery bags. He turns to me. "Sorry about that. I'm surprised Dobbs read the poem out loud. I never meant for you to hear it."

"No worries, man. But still, that doesn't explain anything."

"Yeah, I know." He sighs and shakes his head. "God, I can be such an idiot. Okay, let's see if I can explain this without sounding like a complete jerk. Saturday, when we met on the Drag, I was feeling pretty down. I wanted to find something, you know, to write in my book. And there you were, playing that song. You helped me out. Does that make sense?"

"Um, yeah, I think so."

"And when you gave me your Kinks shirt," he says, "I don't know, it just meant a lot, that's all."

Will looks down and gently kicks one of the grocery bags. Inside, I see a ratty old sweater; next to it, an alarm clock. It occurs to me that the bags are Will's makeshift suitcases, and what's inside is all he owns. I remember what Hawk said: *Take care of Will.*

"Noah! Hey! Come on, we're going to miss our bus!" It's Carson. He's standing near the front of the school, waving both arms over his head like a lunatic.

"Listen," I say to Will. "Where are you staying now?"

"Nowhere, really. I was sleeping on Hawk's sofa, but that got messy, and now he's . . ."

"In jail?" I say.

"Yeah. He'll be out soon, but even so, staying with him is complicated. My social worker's been trying to find me a place, but so far there aren't any takers."

"No *takers*? Dude, they can't just leave you out on the street."

"True. I suppose I could drive around all night with my

41

social worker while she begs for an empty bed, or I could fend for myself. Which is fine with me. I've done it before. I can do it again."

Of all things, a Bible verse pops into my head. *I was hungry, and you gave me something to eat. I was thirsty, and you gave me something to drink. I was a stranger, and you took me in.* Words from the top man himself—Jesus. One thing I know for sure is that my dad would never turn Will away. It's against his religion.

I reach down and grab one of Will's bags. "Be right there, man!" I yell to Carson. "Come on, Will. Let's go. You're with us now."

† † †

The first thing we do is make a pit stop at Carson's. The three of us are starved, and his refrigerator is always chock-full of the best food. "Let's see what we've got," Carson says, rummaging through his freezer. "Gourmet tomato-and-olive pizza, fried mozzarella sticks, chicken quesadillas . . . What do you guys feel like having?"

"All three," I say, turning on the oven. I chug down a tall glass of milk, pour one for Will, and grab a bag of chips from the pantry. Normally Carson's mom likes to wait on us hand and foot, but she plays tennis Monday afternoons and won't be back until six.

I offer Will the chips. Carefully, he plucks one out like it's made of glass, takes a bite, and chews slowly. His eyes scan the white leather sofa, plush carpeting, and big-screen TV in the adjoining room. He's been pretty quiet since the bus ride, and I'm beginning to wonder if it was a mistake bringing him here. Carson's house can be intimidating. "This place is amazing," he says. "I can't believe you live here."

Carson dumps the frozen contents of the boxes onto two metal trays and shoves them into the oven. "Yeah, well, the DPCP really enjoys his creature comforts. What can I say?"

"The DP . . . what?"

"DPCP. Short for Demon-Possessed Capitalist Pig. His father's nickname," I explain. Immediately after saying this, I wish I could take it back. Will would probably give his right arm to *have* a father. And I don't think he'd mind the capitalist part either.

Will doesn't seem offended at all. He laughs. "Hey, that's pretty funny."

"Yeah, but what makes it even funnier," Carson says, "is that Noah's father is the Bible Answer Guy. We're quite a pair, huh?"

I want to smack Carson around for bringing this up. I mean, sure, Will's probably going to find out sooner or later about my father's occupation, but honestly, it would be less embarrassing if my dad was our high school janitor or the neighborhood garbage man.

"Wait a minute," Will says. "Do you mean *the* Bible Answer Guy? As in, the guy on the radio?"

"The one and only," Carson says.

I shove a chip into my mouth and glare at Carson.

"Oh, man, wait till Doomsday hears *this*," Will says, cracking a huge smile. "He's gonna go nuts. He *loves* that guy. I mean, you know, your father. Listens to his show all the time."

"Who's Doomsday?" Carson asks.

"A friend of mine," Will says. "You've seen him. He's that old homeless dude who hangs out on the Drag—the one who preaches and wears signs like 'Repent, for the End Is Near.'"

"Him?"

"Yeah. He's kind of crazy, but he's all right. He looks out for me. Quindlan, too. He's the other guy, the younger one with the mangy dog. All three of us are friends. You'll have to meet them. But, Noah, Doomsday's gonna kiss your feet when he finds out who your dad is."

I snort and shake my head.

"What?" Will says, smiling. "You don't believe me?"

"No, it's not that. I just don't like religious fanatics. I have to live with one."

"So you're a heathen?" Will teases.

"Maybe. Yeah."

"Well, from what I've heard, your dad doesn't seem *so* bad. Like once, he answered a question about the prodigal son, and I thought he was right on. Of course, he probably thinks all gays and abortionists and Muslims are going to hell—"

"Exactly," I say.

Will shrugs. "Hey, I'm sure Doomsday believes that stuff too. I try not to hold it against him. Honestly, I think they're all brainwashed."

"Yeah, they're brainwashed," I say. "But still, people have to think for themselves. I mean, I've heard that shit all my life, but I don't agree with it."

Will studies me. "So you're cool with gay people?"

44

"Sure, why not?"

Carson glances back and forth between the two of us. There's a strange look on his face. He clears his throat. "Hey, Will, when are you gonna introduce us to Doomsday and Quindlan? I've always wanted to meet some crazy street people."

Will laughs. I join in.

"I'm serious!" Carson protests. "It's like this whole other subculture that I know nothing about. I mean, how *could* I, living *here*?"

"He's got a point," I say.

"Well, if I were you, Carson," Will says, "I'd be careful around Doomsday. He saw you on the Drag when you were supposed to be witnessing to the lost, but instead you were staring at that cute girl's ass."

Carson's mouth falls open. "Oh, come on! It was *that* obvious?"

"Yep," Will says. "In fact, you were Doomsday's inspiration. He preached a wicked sermon on the sins of lust and fornication."

"Carson's specialties," I add. "Well, the lust part. He's still working on fornication."

"Har-har, very funny."

After we eat, Will insists on washing the dishes. I pluck a dishrag from the counter and begin to dry. When we're done, Will says, "Hey, Carson, do I have time to take a shower before your folks get home? It's been a while." He takes a whiff of his armpit. "Jeez, I stink."

"Oh, sure, man. Go ahead. The bathroom's right down the hall." When Will's halfway there, Carson says, "Hey, wait, toss me your clothes. We'll wash them along with your other stuff."

Will hesitates for a moment, glances at me, then pulls off his Kinks shirt and tosses it to Carson. His cheeks are pink. Strangely, he looks embarrassed. "Thanks," he says. "Clean clothes would be great." He strips down; hands Carson his jeans, his boxers and a pair of socks; and walks silently, bare-assed, to the bathroom.

"There are plenty of towels in there," Carson calls. "And soap, shampoo, everything you need." Without looking back, Will raises a hand, walks into the bathroom, and shuts the door.

Carson and I head to the laundry room and dump Will's clothes, along with the contents of Will's grocery bags, into the washing machine. Carson is unusually quiet. Finally he says, "So, Will's gay, huh?"

"What? No." I measure out the detergent and pour it into the running water.

Carson stares at me for a while and shakes his head. "You're really dense, Noah. I mean, haven't you noticed the way he looks at you?"

"Shut up. And no, I haven't."

"Well, for me, everything just came together. Will felt weird stripping down in front of you. I could tell."

"So? Maybe he's shy, self-conscious."

"Shy? Come on, Noah. Put the pieces together. Will approached you on the Drag. You told him you liked poetry. You dug his Robert Frost tattoo. You played him a Lead Belly song. You gave him your Kinks shirt, for godsakes. He's still wearing it. Are you *that* blind? The dude's got a crush on you."

I shake my head. "You're freaking nuts, Carson, you know that?"

"Am I?"

Suddenly I feel light-headed, off balance. I think about the poem Will wrote about me. How he reacted when I asked him why so much depended upon *me*. I walk to the living room and plop onto the sofa. A few minutes later, Carson joins me.

"I didn't know you were homophobic," Carson says.

"I'm not."

"Well, you seem a little freaked."

"Wouldn't you be?"

Carson laughs. "I don't think so. Look, Noah, it's no big deal. Will knows you're straight. It's *obvious*. You're a baseball player, an ex-jock. You *exude* testosterone."

I roll my eyes. "You are seriously pissing me off."

"And besides, you told him about Aubrey. He knows you're hopelessly in love with her. Will needs a friend, that's all. Now he's got two of them. Me and you. Besides, now you can put your whole I-don't-agree-with-any-of-that-shit speech into practice."

Carson's grinning at me like an idiot. I can't take it anymore, so I get up, plow through the kitchen, and head outside to the back patio. I hold on to the wood railing, steadying myself, and after breathing some fresh air, I begin to feel a little better. I stare up at the clouds. Is Carson right? Is Will gay? Is he into me? If so, does it matter? I've known girls who've had crushes on me. Well, a few. And we're still friends. So why is this different? *Am* I homophobic?

A few minutes later, Carson joins me on the deck. "Let me ask you something, Noah. You like Will, right? I mean, as a friend?"

"Yeah, of course."

"Okay. Everything's cool. He'll get over you. I mean, really, Noah, you're not *that* irresistible."

"Thanks."

"Come on, forget about this. Let's go tune up our guitars."

Later, as I'm loading Will's clothes into the dryer, he emerges from the bathroom with a towel wrapped around his waist. I look away.

"Wait right there, Will," Carson says. "I've got just the thing." He runs to his parents' bedroom and returns carrying a plush green robe. "Here you go. The DPCP's finest bathrobe. The color of money. Never been worn." He rips off the tag and studies it. "What do you know? It's from Neiman Marcus. A steal at two hundred and fifty bucks."

"Dude, I can't wear that," Will says.

"Of course you can. My dad's got ten others just like it. He'd never even know the difference."

Reluctantly, Will slips his arms into the robe and ties a knot at the waist. "I look ridiculous," he says.

I nod. "Sorry, but yeah, you do."

"No way, it's perfect. Come on." Carson gives Will a little push toward the living room. I follow. He points to his father's favorite lounge chair. "Now, take a seat upon His Majesty's throne, and Noah and I will serenade you. Your clothes are in the dryer. They'll be ready when we're done."

Carson and I grab our mikes and amps from the closet and carry them into the living room. I'm still feeling a little weird about a guy having a crush on me, so I avoid eye contact with Will, wondering why I didn't pick up on the clues—the ones that were obvious to Carson. Or maybe I did? I just don't know. The whole thing is confusing.

Carson hands me my guitar. "Okay, let's do it," he says. "No covers. We're gonna play our original songs. Will, you're the judge. Let us know if we suck or if we're ready for the Austin music scene."

"All right," Will says. "And just so you know, I'm a tough critic. I won't kiss your asses if I think you suck."

"Fair enough," Carson says.

Carson cranks up his amp and begins with his political masterpiece, "Flesh-Eating Zombies," which is supposed to be a satire about American imperialism. The song makes absolutely no sense, but I figure if I play my guitar loudly enough, Will won't be able to hear the god-awful lyrics. It seems to work. After that, we harmonize on some bluesy folk tunes, and last I perform my favorite—an acoustic piece called "Devil Inside My Head." It's got a long harmonica solo. While I play and sing and blow on my harp, I begin to feel fairly normal again. I guess it's the music, which always seems to calm me down. When I'm finished, I look at Will. He smiles appreciatively. Carson's right. Everything's cool. At least, I hope so.

"So, what do you think?" Carson asks Will.

"Honestly, I think you guys are ready for a downtown gig. Have you ever been to the Red Room?"

"Never heard of it," Carson says.

"Oh, we've got to go, then. It's this really cool under-ground club on Seventh and Neches. All ages. It caters to a gay crowd, but there are plenty of straight people who go too. Are you guys . . . okay with that?"

"Oh, yeah," Carson says. "No problem."

Will looks at me. "How about you, Noah?"

"Um, sure, that's fine." My voice cracks a little. I imagined hot *girls* falling all over me and Carson at our first gig. Not hot *guys*. But I suppose beggars can't be choosers.

Will smiles. "Great. I've done some poetry slams there, and I've written a few songs for Kevin Watson. He's a guitarist who plays there most Friday nights."

"Cool. Will we get to hear him play?" Carson says.

Will shifts in his chair. "If it's all right with you guys, I'd rather not book the gig on the same night Kevin's play-ing. We were, well . . . seeing each other and things didn't work out."

So there it is. Will was seeing a guy. Carson gives me an I-told-you-so look. "We understand, Will," Carson says. "No problem."

"Thanks. Anyway, Rob Ramirez is the owner. He's al-ways looking for new bands. I'll talk to him, introduce you guys. In the meantime, record a few songs this week and he'll listen to the CD. I'm sure he'll invite you to play."

Carson flashes me a goofy grin, and I can't help breaking out into a smile. "Yeah! We're doing it, baby!" Carson yells. "Austin! Here we come!" He falls down on his knees and bows before Will. "We're not worthy, O great one!"

We're all cracking up now—that is, until Carson's father walks through the front door. "What the *hell* is going on?"

Carson looks up. "Dad? Why are *you* home?" A legitimate question. The DPCP's a big-time workaholic and never gets home before eight.

Carson's mom follows right behind. I can tell she's been drinking martinis with her tennis friends, but unfortunately the DPCP is stone-cold sober. "Hi, honey." She waves to Carson and smiles at Will and me. "The car broke down and your father had to pick me up. How'd the interview at Kinkos go?"

The color drains from Carson's face. He opens his mouth, but nothing comes out. He tries to stand but can't get off his knees.

The DPCP's eyes narrow into tiny slits. "You didn't go to the interview, did you? After I set the whole thing up? Talked to the supervisor and vouched for you?"

"Uh, well, you see, I kind of . . . forgot."

"Forgot! I don't believe this." The DPCP's eyes scan the rest of the room. He points to Will. "Who the hell are *you*? And why are you wearing my robe?"

"Dear, don't be rude," Carson's mom says.

Will stands up. "Um, sir, I can explain everything. This isn't your son's fault. You see, I—"

"He's our *friend*, Dad," Carson says. "His name's Will. He needs a place to stay and—"

"Wait a minute. A place to *stay*?" Now the DPCP turns his wrath on me. Until now I've seriously doubted Satan's existence, but looking into Carson's dad's eyes, I'm a true believer. "Okay, now I get it!" he screams. "Those *church* people put you up to this, didn't they? I should have known." He points an accusing finger at Carson. "What'd you do, tell

51

them I've got money? Tell them it's no problem for me to take *strangers* into my own home, who, for all I know, want to rip me off blind? Sorry, no, uh-uh, this is *not* happening!"

This is really getting scary. Carson's dad looks like he's about to have a massive stroke. The vein on his forehead is throbbing.

"No!" I blurt out. "That's not it at all! And besides, Will's staying with me. At my house. We were just about to leave."

It's the first time I've ever stood up to the DPCP, and let me tell you, it feels good. He glances at me, then at Will, and surprisingly looks a little embarrassed about his tirade. For a second, I almost feel sorry for him. Almost. He takes a seat on the sofa and puts his head in his hands. Carson's mom sits beside him and whispers something in his ear.

"I'm sorry about the robe, sir," Will says. "And I didn't take anything from your house. I swear. You can check."

Carson's father sighs deeply. "Whatever. It doesn't matter. Keep the goddamn robe. Just . . . get on your way."

Carson, Will, and I exchange glances. We head to the kitchen and stuff Will's clothes from the dryer back into the grocery bags. Will goes to the bathroom and puts on clean jeans and a T-shirt, and as we're about to walk out the back door, the DPCP pipes up. "Oh, no! Not you, Carson. You're staying right here. You're going to call Kinkos and explain to the supervisor why you didn't show up today. And then you're going to *beg* for another interview."

Carson's about to mouth off to his father, but I stop him. "Dude, *don't.* Just do what he tells you. I've got everything under control. I'll call you later, okay?"

Will puts a hand on Carson's shoulder. "Noah's right," he says. "Listen to your dad. And thanks for everything. Really. I had a great time."

Carson looks up. His eyes are glassy. He's holding back tears. "I hate the son of a bitch."

"Nah," Will says. "You don't hate him. You just think you do. Anyway, remember, the three of us are going to the Red Room real soon. You guys are gonna *rock*."

{seven}

"LOOK, DADDY, it's Noah! And he brought a friend! Now we can play a *real* game!"

Will and I just stepped into my backyard. On the small field of grass, right beyond the patio, a baseball game is in session, with Melanie up at bat and my dad on the pitcher's mound. When my father sees us, he races to the shed, tosses us each a glove, and says, "Spread out, boys. She's hitting solid today. There's a man on first and third. No outs." Like I said before, baseball's my father's other religion. And let me tell you, he's a fanatic.

"Cool." Will slips on the glove and gives it a firm punch. He doesn't even question the invisible men on base or the fact that my dad didn't bother to say hello. He runs out to center field and I take first. Meanwhile Melanie swings her bat hard, warming up for a homer. I've got to hand it to the kid. Most girls her age play softball, but not my sister. For her, it's baseball or nothing. And not only is she the best hitter on her team, she's one fearless catcher.

Right now she's a little wound up and misses the first pitch. "Take it easy, Mel," my dad says. "Concentrate. Wait for the ball. Remember? The secret is *patience* and *self-control*."

Two fruits of the Holy Spirit. It's amazing how my dad's been brainwashing Melanie and me with Bible verses since birth. Like just the other day, when I was weed-whacking, he made a joke, saying, "Cursed is the ground . . . by the sweat of your brow you will eat your food." Hilarious, right? I'm on the road to recovery, but I'm still in need of a serious deprogramming.

On the next pitch, Melanie connects and sends the ball flying over Will's head. "Whoa, would you look at that!" Will yells. He scrambles to get it, but by the time he does, she's home.

"Yay! That's three runs in!" Melanie grabs the bat and gives home plate a whack. The kid is a major show-off, but since she's cute, no one really minds. Including me. She follows up with a single and a triple, and after she delivers another big hit to the outfield, my dad says, "Okay, Melanie, remember our deal?" He taps his watch. "It's six o'clock. Time to go inside and do your homework."

"Aw, already?"

"Yes, you know the rules."

Will jogs toward us and tosses the ball to my father. "Hey, Melanie, those were some hits! And what do you know?" He points to her hat. "You're an Angels fan!"

She beams. "Yeah! Are you?"

"Definitely. That's my home team. I moved to Austin when I was about your age, but I'm originally from L.A."

"Really? Hey, I've got a ball signed by Orlando Cabrera. You want to see it?"

"Sure."

"Is that okay, Daddy? Can I show Noah's friend the ball, and then do my homework?"

"Um, okay, honey." My father smiles and holds out his hand to Will. "Sorry, I guess I got carried away with the game and didn't introduce myself. I'm John Nordstrom, Noah's dad."

"I know," Will says as they shake. "I've heard your radio show many times. And I have a friend who's a huge fan. I'd recognize your voice anywhere. My name's Will."

My dad is flattered, but since humility is one of his favorite virtues, he just nods. "Nice to meet you, Will."

I want to say, *Congratulations, Dad. You officially met a gay person.* But I don't think that'll go over too well.

"Come on!" Melanie grabs Will's hand and pulls him toward the house. "I've got all the Angels trading cards too!"

Suddenly my father and I are alone. It's weird being here in the backyard with him. Before I got sent to the Rock, when I was playing for McCallum High, he'd always drag me back here to practice my pitching. I hate to admit it, but my father taught me how to throw my infamous curveball—the one no one could hit last season.

"So . . . ," my dad says, "is Will a new friend from church?"

It takes a lot of willpower, but I somehow manage *not* to roll my eyes. I swear, if I had a redneck gunslinger for a friend, as long as he went to King of Glory Christian Center, well,

that would be just fine. "No, Dad. Will's not from church. I met him on the Drag Saturday. It turns out he goes to my school. In fact, I was going to ask you a favor. You see—"

"Your school? You mean he goes to the *Rock*?"

"Well, yeah, but—"

He shakes his head. "Noah, you know how I feel about your choice of friends lately, and if this boy goes to the Rock, well, I can only imagine what kind of trouble—"

"Dad," I say, "Will needs a place to stay. He's a foster kid, and right now he's got nowhere to go."

My father's quiet for a while. "Nowhere at all? Are you sure about that?"

"Yeah. His social worker's been looking, but she can't find him a home. I'm pretty sure he's been sleeping out in the woods."

"The woods?" He sighs. "Well, we can't have that. I'll talk to your mother. If she says it's all right, he can stay with us this evening. I'll get in touch with some people tomorrow. We'll figure something out."

"Thanks, Dad."

It's a done deal. My mother would never turn Will away. In fact, she's probably already invited him to stay for dinner. I hand my father my glove, the one he bought me for Christmas last year, right before baseball season. He'd broken it in for me, oiled it and everything. He runs his fingers over the leather and sighs again. "Come on, let's see if Mom needs help in the kitchen."

Inside, my mom is slicing mushrooms. "Noah, your friend Will is having dinner with us. Why don't you set the table?" She hands me a stack of dishes, and my father a hunk

of cheese. "John, you can grate the Parmesan. And remember, use a delicate touch."

My dad shakes his head and smiles. My mom's the only person who can get away with bossing him around. As he slides the hunk of cheese over the grater, he says, "Laura, it turns out Will needs a place to sleep tonight. He's in foster care, and apparently has nowhere to stay. I'll see what I can do about the situation tomorrow. Anyway, is that okay with you? If it's not, I can—"

"Of course it's okay." She turns to me. "Noah? Is Will completely alone? No family at all?"

"Well, his parents died when he was ten. They were killed in a car wreck. Since then, he's been in different foster homes, and bounced around a lot."

"Oh." She dumps the mushrooms into a pan of sizzling butter and frowns. "How sad. He seems like such a nice boy. John, when you're done grating the cheese, you can put clean sheets on the guest bed. And don't forget the pillowcases. They're in the linen closet."

"Yes, dear."

When we're all seated at the dinner table, my dad bows his head. "Lord, we thank you for this wonderful meal, and for our guest, Will. Please bless our fellowship tonight, and our conversation around the dinner table. In Jesus's name we pray, Amen."

Short and sweet. Glory, hallelujah.

"Amen," Will says. He opens his eyes and looks around. "Thank you so much for inviting me, Mr. and Mrs. Nordstrom. The food smells delicious."

Will sounds like he's kissing up to my parents, but the

truth is he's totally sincere. And starving. My mom passes him the basket of French bread and he rips off a huge piece.

"We're glad you're here," she says. "And you're more than welcome to spend the night. John's going to look into a few possibilities for you tomorrow. He'll try and get you settled."

"Oh, thank you, but please don't go to any trouble. Really, I'll be fine."

"It's no trouble at all," my dad says.

Melanie passes Will the spaghetti; he heaps it onto his plate. She laughs. "You're pretty hungry, huh?"

"Oh, yeah. I'm always hungry."

She hands him the pot of sauce and watches as he ladles it on top of the spaghetti. For her enjoyment, he shovels a huge forkful of food into his mouth and chews.

"So, Will, tell us about yourself," my dad says. "Are you a junior?"

Will swallows his food and takes a sip of water. "Senior," he says. "I'll be eighteen pretty soon. When I graduate, I'm planning to head out to L.A. Well, if I can save up enough money. I've got a friend there, and hopefully a job lined up."

"Really? That's wonderful," my mom says. "What kind of job?"

Will hesitates for a moment. "Uh, it's with the L.A. Youth Connection. They work with foster kids. A guy I know runs a program for . . . well, for teens with special needs. He wants to raise awareness, promote tolerance, provide counseling, stuff like that. If he can work something out, I'd be his assistant. It wouldn't pay much, but that's okay. I'd be doing something I like. Something I believe in."

"Sounds like a worthy cause," my dad says. He takes a

bite of French bread, chews, and swallows. "But tell me, Will, does this group also provide spiritual guidance for these teens? And maybe a good church for them to attend?"

I stop chewing and glare at my dad. I want to throttle him.

"Because I feel that's very important," he goes on. "It's noble to want to help, but in my opinion what these teens really need is God."

"Maybe they already have God," Will says.

"Well, yes, of course that's a possibility, but considering their backgrounds . . ." My father trails off. The Bible Answer Guy has officially put his foot in his mouth.

Will looks at me.

I set down my fork. "So what are you trying to say, Dad? That the L.A. Youth Connection should hire a group of evangelicals? Make sure all the foster kids go through the five-point plan of salvation?"

"Noah, please," my dad says. "That's not what I'm—"

"Or maybe we should send them all free Bibles, and make them listen to your show?"

"That's. Enough. Noah."

While my father glares at me, Will says, "Listen, I'm sorry, Mr. Nordstrom. I didn't mean to cause a problem. And I should probably explain something. You see, the group I hope to be working with promotes tolerance for gay teens."

Oh, great. Here we go.

My dad blinks. "I see."

My mother glances around nervously. She reaches across the table, takes Will's hand, and gives it a squeeze. "Well, I think that's just wonderful, Will. And I want you to know our church welcomes *everyone*."

"That's for sure," Melanie says. "Last Sunday there was this smelly guy talking to himself, sitting right behind me. I'm pretty sure he had *lice*. They didn't even kick *him* out."

Will laughs. He pushes some spaghetti around on his plate. "Mr. Nordstrom? I . . . hear what you're saying, but don't evangelical Christians believe that homosexuality is a sin?"

"Well, yes," my father says. "But we're all sinners—in need of the Lord." He pauses for a moment and clears his throat. "Will, I should explain something too. You see, the problem I have with a secular group like L.A. Youth Connection is they assume gay teens are certain of their sexual orientation. My question is, how can a teenager be sure he's gay at such a young age? Maybe he's confused and needs counseling?"

I can see where this conversation is going, and I don't like it. Will takes a deep breath. I nudge his foot under the table and shake my head. *Don't, Will. Don't open this can of worms.*

"I know what gay is," Melanie says. "It's when a boy wants to marry another boy. That's *so* weird."

Will chokes down a laugh. "Well, it *is* different, Melanie, but it's not *that* weird. Not as weird as, say, space monkeys or mutant ninja turtles."

Melanie thinks this one over. "I guess."

"Anyway, to answer your question, Mr. Nordstrom, most gay kids know they're gay from a pretty young age. The problem is when people tell them it's wrong. Or say it's a sin. That's usually when the kids need counseling. L.A. Youth Connection believes that gay teens need to accept themselves for who they are."

"Wait a minute," Melanie says. "Are *you* gay, Will?"

"Melanie!" my mom scolds.

"What? It's just a question."

Before Will can answer, I say, "Mel, enough already! Can we just eat dinner? Can we stop talking about this?"

Will looks down at his plate.

"I think that's a good idea, Noah," my mother says. "Please, let's enjoy dinner. And mind your own business, Melanie."

Melanie frowns and sticks her tongue out at me. I give her the evil eye.

"I apologize, Mr. Nordstrom," Will says. "I shouldn't have brought any of that up."

"No, it's fine," my dad says. "No harm done."

My father studies me from across the table as we eat in silence. In defiance, I stare right back at him.

Suddenly he clears his throat. "Well, I certainly hope you make it back to L.A., Will. It sounds like the perfect job for you."

Yeah, let's hope he moves back to L.A., right, Dad? Out of sight, out of mind.

"Thank you, sir."

After dinner, Will offers to clean up. My mother protests, but he insists. "Please, it's the least I can do, Mrs. Nordstrom. I'd like to help."

Finally she gives in, heads to the adjoining family room,

and takes a seat on the sofa next to my dad. He turns on the news. Meanwhile Melanie runs upstairs to finish her homework.

Will and I work together—I clear the table while he loads the dishwasher—and we don't say much. As he rinses off the last plate, he says, "Noah? Are you sure you're cool with me being here?"

"Of course. Why wouldn't I be?"

"I don't know. Your parents are really nice, and Melanie's great, but things got a little tense over dinner. Plus, you seem kind of freaked. Maybe I'd better leave?"

"No. You're not leaving. And I'm not freaked."

I hear my mother gasp from the family room. I look up, peer more closely at the TV, and see a familiar face on the screen. A mug shot. It's Melanie's former Sunday school teacher, Warren Banks. Below the photo are the words *Suspect in Murder of Gay Teen*. I shut the refrigerator, walk into the room, and motion for Will to join me. Instead, he stands there frozen, watching from a distance.

"John?" my mother says. "I don't understand. How could this be?"

I turn up the volume. The newscaster continues.

"Warren Banks, suspect in the murder of Austin teenager Kyle Lester, is a former member of King of Glory Christian Center—a local independent church. Earlier this year, Banks left King of Glory and joined an Austin branch of the Westboro Baptist Church, whose main headquarters is in Topeka, Kansas. The Westboro church is widely known for its Web site, God Hates Fags dot-com. Banks is twenty-five years old and a former employee at a software company."

I glance back at Will. His eyes are glued to the TV.

Now, beside the mug shot of Warren Banks, News 8 is showing a clip of a group from the Westboro Baptist Church marching and holding up signs that say GOD HATES FAGS! FAGS HATE GOD! AIDS CURES FAGS! AMERICA IS DOOMED!

The newscaster goes on. "According to police reports, Kyle Lester was last seen alive with Warren Banks outside Urban Legend, a downtown bar on Sixth Street. The owner, Herb Underwood, claims that Banks was a regular customer. Banks has pleaded not guilty to the murder, and right now police are awaiting DNA results."

I take a closer look at Banks on the TV screen. The only time I ever spoke to the guy was when I picked up Melanie from Sunday school class. Drily, he'd tell me the Bible verse she was supposed to memorize for the following week so she could get a star next to her name. To me, he was just another church nerd. Never in a million years would I have thought, *Murderer*.

"But what complicates matters further in this case is that another body was found this morning near Town Lake—a teenage boy who had been in the foster care system. Due to his age, his name is not being released. According to police, this boy had been killed in the same manner as Kyle Lester. Apparently he'd been strangled with a rope, which was found at the crime scene. A cross had been carved into the flesh of his chest. A note had been left using letters cut from newspaper—part of a Bible verse condemning homosexuality, one similar to the note found with Kyle Lester. 'Leviticus 20:13—If a man lieth with mankind, they shall surely be put to death; their blood shall be upon them.'"

My stomach plummets. Another murder. Another gay foster kid. It could have been Will.

"Coroners are determining the time of the teenager's death. If the boy was killed before the arrest of Warren Banks, Banks will be a suspect in this murder as well."

News 8 goes on to their next story, something about a hazing at a UT frat party.

I walk over to Will. He's staring straight ahead, the color drained from his face. "Will, are you okay?"

"I don't know. I just . . . I can't believe this is happening."

"Me neither." I take a deep breath. "There's something I should tell you. That guy, Warren Banks, the one they arrested, he used to go to our church."

Will looks at me. Except for the TV droning, the room is deathly quiet. My parents are sitting there like statues. "And remember when I asked you about Kyle Lester?" I say. "Here's why: a week before his murder there was a crazy guy calling in on my dad's show, saying all this crap about gay people, and—"

"I know."

"You do?"

"Yeah. I heard the show with Doomsday."

My mother turns around. She's crying. "Will, please, I want you to know that *our* church, what we believe, it's nothing like that horrible Westboro Baptist hate group. I mean, there's just no excuse—"

"I understand, Mrs. Nordstrom, really. You don't need to explain."

My dad puts a hand on my mother's shoulder. There's a pained expression on his face. I know Kyle's murder still haunts him. Now another boy is dead. And now he's facing Will—a living, breathing gay teenager standing in his own kitchen. Someone he just shared a meal with. If he had to take that call over again, what would his answer be?

"Mrs. Nordstrom?" Will says. "Is it okay if I chill out in the guest room? I'd like to be alone for a while."

"Of course, Will. Go right ahead. Let us know if you need anything."

Will picks up his grocery bags.

"Hey, I'll come by later, dude," I say. "Maybe we can play a game of chess or something? Take your mind off things?"

"Yeah. Sure. Thanks, Noah."

After Will closes the door of the guest room, I take a seat opposite my parents.

My mom lowers the volume on the TV. "John, this is crazy. That guy was Melanie's Sunday school teacher. And to think we had no clue."

My dad nods slowly. "Yes, well, obviously Warren Banks is *very* disturbed and *very* good at hiding it. Still, it's hard to believe no one from King of Glory caught on. They do background checks on all the people in the children's ministry, so apparently his record was clean." He sighs. "At least they've got him now. It won't happen again."

"I think we should keep in mind that he's just a suspect," my mom says. "He's not necessarily guilty. Although it certainly seems that way."

"There's something I don't get," I say. "On the news, they said Warren Banks was a regular customer at Urban Legend. So doesn't that mean . . . ?"

"That Banks is homosexual?" my father says. "It's certainly

possible. He could have been fighting his . . . well, his demons, so to speak, projected his struggle on others, and become violent, but it's also just as likely that he was a stalker waiting for the right victim. Someone like Kyle, and now this other boy. Whatever the case, they're both heinous hate crimes."

I sit there for a while, thinking about how screwed up all this is. Demons? Christian gay-bashers? If you ask me, John Lennon was right. Imagine a world with no religion. Maybe *that's* heaven.

"Dad? Do you think that's him? Do you think Warren Banks is the caller from your show?"

He sighs deeply. "There's no way to tell, Noah. If you remember, he disguised his voice with some sort of digital device. The police have all the audiotapes of my show. They weren't able to make a match."

"I know it's him," I say. "I just do. When you put it together—what he said on your show, and the fact that Kyle was killed one week after he stopped calling. And now we find out he was a member of that crazy church."

My dad is quiet for a long time. Finally he says, "Noah, even if Warren Banks was the caller, I didn't have the ability to stop his crimes. Yes, what he said was hateful, but you know what the Bible says about homosexuality." He glances toward the guest room and lowers his voice. "It doesn't matter that you have a friend who's gay. It's still a sin. Period. I can't pretend that it's not. I'm not going to condone homosexuality on my show."

"Really?" I say. "So let me ask you something, Dad. What if *I* was gay? Your own son. What would you do? Disown me? Throw me out of the house? Damn me to hell?"

"Noah, please," my mother says. "Don't speak to your father that way."

"I'll speak to him however I like. And what about the other Bible verse, Dad? The one that says, 'Do not judge, or you too will be judged.' Do you just toss that one out the window? You're so busy pointing the finger. Have you even bothered to look at yourself?"

I'm seething now. I get up, march to my room, and slam the door. A minute later, Melanie pokes her head in. "Noah, what's wrong? Why are you screaming at Daddy?"

"Go away!"

She makes a face, slams the door, and runs down the stairs. "Mom? Dad? What's the matter with Noah?"

I grab my iPod, stuff the earpieces into my ears, and turn up the volume. I lie down for a while, then pick up my chess set and head for the guest room. I knock. "Will? Hey, is it all right if I come in?"

No answer.

"Will?" I push the door open. "Will?" I look around. He's gone. There's a note on the pillow. I pick it up. Scrawled on the page is the first sentence of Tupac's poem.

Did you hear about the rose that grew from a crack in the concrete? That's me, Noah. The rose. So do me a favor and don't worry. And go easy on your dad. I'll be fine. Thanks for everything.

Will

{eight}

THE NEXT day I'm in PE, bouncing a basketball on the outdoor courts. It's a game of one-on-one against myself. The rest of the class is playing softball, but I'm not in the mood for team sports. Not today. Each time my ball hits the ground, inside my head I hear *God. Hates. Fags. Bounce, bounce. Fags. Hate. God. Bounce, bounce.* I want to scream. I lift the ball, and just as I'm about to shoot, someone calls, "Noah!"

I turn and see Will. He's hiding behind the rear wall of the school, waving me over. I glance around. Coach Cameron is pitching softballs, his back toward me. I toss the basketball and run over to Will.

"Dude, what's going on?" I say. "Why'd you leave last night?"

"Don't worry about that, Noah. It's not a big deal. I had stuff to do."

"Stuff? Like what? Will, the body they found near Town Lake? That could have been *you*."

He takes a deep breath. "Yeah, I know. Look, I don't want you to get involved in this, Noah. I had to split last night because I knew your parents would try to force me to stay. And, well, I couldn't."

"I wish you had. My dad might be an asshole, but he was going to find you a home. He wouldn't have given up until he'd known you were safe."

"I know. But right now, I just . . . I need a friend. Someone to talk to. This whole thing is freaking me out. I'm scared."

"Me too." I glance back at my PE class. Coach Cameron is still pitching softballs. As far as I can tell, no one knows I'm missing. "I've got about twenty minutes. But what about you? Shouldn't you be in class?"

"I called in sick. I'm planning to be sick all week. Last night, after I left your house, I went to talk to the undercover detective I used to work with. He thinks it's best for me to disappear for a while. He's gonna help me out."

"Disappear? But where will you go?"

"Don't worry, I have a place. Anyway, I won't be around for a while, so I wanted to say goodbye. Also, I wanted to give you something."

Will reaches inside his coat, pulls out a leather notebook, and hands it to me. It resembles his book of poetry, but it's newer, less worn. "You can write your songs in there," he says.

I open the book. The pages are blank, except for the inside cover.

Dear Noah,

Let your words slice like a diamond,
a million facets of light.

Your friend,
Will

"Nordstrom! What the hell are you doing over there?" It's Coach Cameron. The snitch beside him is TJ Dumont.

"You'd better go," Will says.

"But—"

"Hurry." Will takes off.

I shove the book into my back pocket and head toward Coach.

"Who was with you?" he says.

"No one."

"Right. Spread your arms and legs."

TJ smirks while Coach pats me down. When Coach gets to my back pocket, he pulls out the book. "What's this?"

"Um, a book," I say.

"Don't be a wiseguy, Nordstrom. I can see it's a book. Why's it in your back pocket during PE?"

I shrug. "Thought I'd take some notes."

"Very funny." He flips through the pages, looking for drugs or razor blades or god knows what, and hands it back to me. "All right. Get back to the courts. Fifty push-ups and a hundred sit-ups. Now!"

When I'm on push-up number twenty-three, TJ Dumont

strolls up behind me and whips the book out of my pocket. I jump up and try to grab it, but it's too late.

"'Dear Noah . . .'" He reads the inscription aloud. The moron pronounces *facets* like *faucets*. "'Your friend, *Will*.'" A grin spreads across his face. "Whoa! Guys! Get a load of this! Nordstrom's a queer! Some *dude* is writing him poetry!"

"Shut up, Dumont. Give me the book."

He holds up a limp wrist, grabs his crotch with his other hand, and makes an obscene gesture. "What were you two faggots doing behind the wall, Nordstrom? Sticking it where the sun don't shine?"

Without even thinking I punch Dumont in the stomach. He falls to the ground. I grab the book.

"Nordstrom!" Coach calls. "All right, that's it! Get your ass to the office! Now!"

While the class looks on in amusement, some clapping, some whistling, I shove the book into my pocket and head toward the door. As I'm walking through the hallway to the main office, I stop in front of a trash can. I hesitate for a moment, then pop the lid, drop in the book, and listen to the quiet thud.

{nine}

MY PUNISHMENT for punching TJ Dumont in the gut is one week of ISS—In-School Suspension, a term the Rock uses to mean torturing students until they succumb to a mental breakdown. Basically you go to a room filled with other offenders and do your work silently, and if you speak one word—even during lunch, when you're trying to gag down a prison soy burger—they give you an extra day of ISS. I've heard that some kids never get out.

Anyway, it's my first day. I'm halfway through my math assignment when someone taps me on the shoulder. I turn around. It's Hawk. He slips into the seat behind me. It's the first time I've seen him since the police handcuffed him in the hallway, since he leaned over and whispered, "Noah, take care of Will."

Beneath the desk he hands me a crumpled, dirt-stained sheet of paper, folded in half. I open it and read:

The Red Room
Next Saturday
Be there
Will

I look at Hawk and mouth, *Where is he? Have you seen him?*

Hawk shakes his head and motions to the front of the room. Slowly, I turn around.

Mr. Briggs is glaring at me. "Is there a problem, Mr. Nordstrom?"

"No, sir. No problem."

"And, Mr. Smith," he says to Hawk, "what are you doing here? I don't have you on the ISS list."

Hawk stands, walks to the front of the room, and hands Briggs a referral paper. Briggs studies it. "Fine, have a seat. You know the rules."

Hawk looks straight ahead when he passes my desk. He takes a seat. I try to concentrate on my math, but I can't. I look at the clock on the wall, ticking away the minutes. I wait for Mr. Briggs to answer a phone call, pour a cup of coffee, scratch an itch—anything. Finally he reaches into his bag and shuffles through some papers. I turn around.

Hawk is gone.

† † †

After school, while Carson and I are waiting for the bus, I show him the note.

"I don't know, man," he says. "I mean, I definitely want to rock out at the Red Room and all, but this is weird. Hawk delivers the note, and then he disappears? Briggs has security search for him and he doesn't show up. I mean, what's going on?"

"I don't know. I wish Will had told me where he'd be hiding. I just want to talk to him, make sure he's all right."

"Hey, Noah?" Carson says. "Are you going to show that note to your father? Let him know Will's been in touch?"

I think this over. "No. Why should I? What good would it do?"

After Will left our house Monday night, my father called Child Protective Services. They told him they would contact Will's social worker and, after twenty-four hours, file a missing persons report. Whether they did, I don't know; I haven't spoken a word to my dad since Will left.

A minute later our bus pulls in. "Hey, Carson, I have an idea about how we might find Will. Do you still have the spare key to the DPCP's old Lexus?"

Carson's got his driver's license, but since he's been such a screwup lately, his dad took his keys away and hasn't let him drive. Luckily Carson made a spare in case of an emergency. Like this one. He grins. "Yeah. It's in my room. Why?"

"Let's take it down to the Drag. We need some answers."

† † †

Carson parks the Lexus on Twentieth and Guadalupe, and together we head to the old Methodist church.

Doomsday is propped up against one of the carved wooden doors, hunched over a tattered book, his lips moving. I peer at the book's cover, expecting a Bible, but it's Walt Whitman's *Leaves of Grass*. Quindlan is lying beside Doomsday on his bedroll, eyes closed, petting his mangy dog and taking in the sun. As we climb the stairs, I hear Doomsday reading aloud to Quindlan.

> *"Scented herbage of my breast,*
> *Leaves from you I glean . . ."*

Suddenly the dog's ears perk up. He lets out a yap. Quindlan sits up; Doomsday stops reading. "Well, well, what do you know?" Quindlan says. "We've got company, Dooms. It's Rasta Man and the Bible Answer Boy."

Doomsday blinks a few times and scratches his beard. The guy's ancient. He gazes at me like he's Moses and I'm the burning bush.

Carson leans over and whispers, "Did that guy just call me *Rasta Man?*"

"Yeah. I guess it's your dreads."

Quindlan stands and holds out a hand to me. He looks to be in his midthirties, and if you didn't know he was homeless, you might think he was a grad student living in one of those hippie co-ops. He's pretty grungy, though, and his dog's got some nasty-looking bald patches. I hesitate for a moment, wondering which communicable disease I'm going to catch if I shake his hand. He chuckles. "Don't worry, Bible Boy, I don't bite. Besides"—he pats the dog's head and grins—"Hercules and I both got our rabies shots last week."

Doomsday bursts out laughing. "You better watch out, boys. That Quindlan, he's a bit of a schizoid."

Quindlan winks at me. My face burns as I shake his hand. "Nice to meet you," I say.

"Same here. We were hoping you'd stop by. Doomsday's your father's biggest fan."

"Nice," I say. "I'll be sure to let my dad know."

Quindlan moves on to Carson, who doesn't look too thrilled about the handshake either. "We saw you here on the Drag last week," Quindlan says to Carson, "playing evangelist and chasing after that pretty girl."

"Yes, we did," Doomsday chimes in, giving Carson the death stare. "If your right eye causes you to sin, pluck it out! Better to lose one part of your body than to have your whole body thrown into hell. Matthew five, twenty-nine."

Carson's speechless. He looks at me.

"Don't mind Doomsday," Quindlan says. "He means well; he just gets carried away sometimes."

Carson leans over and gives me a nudge. "Come on, dude, get on with it."

"Listen, maybe you guys can help us," I say. "We're looking for Will. Do you know where he is?"

"We might," Quindlan says, "but, please, come join us for a while. Doomsday was just finishing a beautiful passage from *Leaves of Grass*. The man reads with such heart."

"Oh, no thanks," I say. "I mean, we'd like to, but we're in kind of a rush."

"Yeah," Carson says. "A big rush."

"Plus," I go on, "we're really worried about Will, so if you could—"

"Will's fine," Quindlan says. "Absolutely fine. And besides, there's always time for poetry. Especially if Doomsday's reading." He gazes up at the UT tower. "Did Will tell you? Doomsday used to be a professor at the college. He taught American literature. In fact, that's how he and Will got to be such good friends. They both love words."

Jeez, maybe Quindlan is a schizoid. "Um, no, he didn't mention that. But if you would just—"

"Please, come, sit down. When Dooms is finished, we'll talk about Will."

I look at Carson and shrug. It's not like we have much of a choice. We take seats on the ground opposite Doomsday. Immediately Quindlan's mangy dog jumps into Carson's lap and starts licking his face. "Hey, what do you know?" Quindlan says. "Hercules likes you."

"Yeah, lucky me," Carson says.

Doomsday continues reading from *Leaves of Grass.*

> *"Tomb-leaves, body-leaves,*
> *growing up above me, above death . . ."*

I have to admit, the guy's got perfect diction, a lilting cadence, and just the right amount of emotion. If you closed your eyes and breathed through your mouth to avoid the occasional whiff of rank air, you might think you were in a college classroom.

When Doomsday is finished, he sighs deeply and closes the book. He holds out a hand to me, and this time I make sure I don't hesitate. We shake. "It's a pleasure to meet you, Noah. Your father is a great man. A modern-day John the

Baptist. A true hero." He tightens his grip and looks into my eyes. "We need to talk. I'd love to hear your opinion on end-time prophecy."

"Well, actually, I don't know anything about that." I wiggle my hand free and turn to Quindlan. "You said Will was okay. We really need to see him. Please, can you tell us where he is now?"

Doomsday peers at me. "Why, *exactly*, do you want to see Will?"

"Because we're friends. He hasn't been at school, and with everything that's going on, you know, with the two foster kids who were murdered, we're worried."

Under his breath, Doomsday mutters to Quindlan, "Don't do it, don't do it, don't do it."

Quindlan pats his knee. "Calm down, Dooms."

Doomsday exhales loudly, waves Quindlan away, and goes back to his book. He mumbles, "'Resist the devil and he will flee from you.'"

"Come on, boys, follow me," Quindlan says. He motions for me and Carson to get up. We do. As he leads us to the other side of the church, Hercules trails after Carson, whimpering.

"Okay, I'm going to draw you a map that will take you to Will," Quindlan says. "Here, turn around, Noah." He plucks a pen and paper from his pocket. I lean over, and he uses my back for a hard surface. He begins to draw.

Meanwhile Carson stoops down and pets Hercules. He peers at Doomsday, who's still hunched over his book in the distance. "Quindlan?" Carson says. "Were you joking before, about Doomsday being a professor?"

Quindlan stops drawing. "That's no joke. Doomsday taught at UT for almost twenty years."

"So what happened?" Carson says.

"Well, after a while the past finally caught up with him. When he was a student here, his fiancée was killed by the UT sniper."

I turn around. "Oh my God, you're kidding."

"Sadly, no." Quindlan points to the tower where the sniper, Charles Whitman, shot several students back in the late sixties. Carson and I both know the story. Just about everyone in Austin does. "Her name was Mary. She died right here on Guadalupe. It's almost like Doomsday's been keeping vigil."

"That's heavy," Carson says.

"Yeah, most people think Doomsday's just some crazy old man. The truth is, most of us around here have a story to tell."

"What about you?" Carson says. "What's your story?"

"Me? Oh, nothing, really. Just down on my luck. Lost my job a few years back and things kind of spiraled downward fast. Came to Austin from up north about six months ago and met Doomsday and Will. I decided to stay put for a while. They're like my family now. Anyway, let me finish this map."

"Sure." I turn around. When Quindlan is done, he hands me the paper. I take a look. It's a map of the Barton Creek Greenbelt.

"Will's at the greenbelt?"

"Yep. Camping out. It's a good place to be lost."

The sketch is meticulous. Every gate and milestone is marked. A small X shows where Will has set up camp.

"I just didn't expect that," I say. "Anyway, thank you."

"Noah, before you leave, I need to talk with you." Quindlan glances at Carson. "Alone, if that's okay."

"Um, sure," I say. "Hey, Carson, I'll be right back."

Carson nods and takes a seat on the church steps; Hercules happily jumps onto his lap. "No worries, man. Go ahead. Me and Hercules will chill out here for a while."

Quindlan leads me to the side entrance of the church, opens the door, and ushers me inside. We take seats on the back pew. There are a few people praying in the front row, but the place is mostly empty and eerily quiet. I'm wondering what Quindlan can't say in front of Carson.

He shifts in his seat. "Noah, this might be a little awkward for you, but are you aware of how Will feels about you?"

"Uh, well, if you mean . . ."

He nods.

"Yeah, I figured it out. Actually, Carson caught on first and told me."

"And you're okay with that?"

"Well, it's the first time a *guy's* had a crush on me, but I think I can handle it. Why?"

"I just wanted to make sure. Will's a sensitive kid, and I don't want to see him get hurt. Anyway, I'm glad you're open-minded. Not everyone is. Like Doomsday, for example. He and Will are friends, but Will doesn't share the fact that he's gay. There's no point, really."

"But he shared it with you?"

"Yes. And he told me what happened at your house Monday night—the way your father reacted."

"Right. My dad. Chased him off."

"Well, yes and no. Will's pretty independent. He has a hard time accepting help from anyone. Plus, he was really upset about what he heard on the news that night. About the second murder. He wanted to find out who the boy was. As it turned out, he knew this kid too. It shook him up badly."

"Oh, God. Who was it?"

"His name was Paul Mateo. He was a kid Will knew when they were younger. Will said Paul used to get picked on a lot. It's really sad. Seems like this killer not only hates gay people, but preys on helpless kids too. Hopefully the guy they arrested is the one."

"Warren Banks," I say, picturing his mug shot on TV. There's a sick feeling in the pit of my stomach. "He used to go to our church. He was my sister's Sunday school teacher."

Quindlan nods. "I know. Will told me." There's an uneasy silence between us. "Noah, I understand how you feel about your father. I grew up in a family like yours."

"Really?"

"Yeah. Before, when Carson asked what my story was, I didn't tell you. I have a hard time talking about it. You see, my father was the founder of an evangelical ministry called God's Warriors. His mission was to bring the gospel to teenage gang members in the South Bronx. And, well, he did a lot of good things, helped kids get off drugs and off the streets, but he was pretty hard-core about his beliefs. When he found out my brother was gay, he basically wrote him off.

A year later we found my brother in the bathtub. He'd slit his wrists and bled to death. He was only seventeen. After that, I left home. I was eighteen."

I look at Quindlan. "That's terrible. I'm so sorry. God, I wish . . ."

"Things were different? Me too."

"I'm just so sick of Christians, or people who *call* themselves Christians, being so hateful," I say. "They judge everyone who doesn't fit into their stupid mold. So, if you're different, if you're gay, well, then it's a sickness, a wrong choice, a sin. It's so screwed up."

"I agree," Quindlan says.

"That night, before Will left, I got so angry. I challenged my father. I said, 'What would you do if *I* was gay, Dad?' He couldn't even answer me."

"I understand, Noah. Some people choose their beliefs, no matter how wrong they are, over their own families."

"Yeah." I look at Quindlan. "I'm really sorry about your brother."

"Thanks."

Suddenly I feel a stab of guilt, remembering how good it felt to punch TJ Dumont, watch him fall on his ass. All because he called me a queer. Why didn't I just ignore the moron and walk away? Why didn't I keep Will's book instead of throwing it into the trash?

"Come on," Quindlan says. "You'll want to find Will before it gets dark."

{ten}

CARSON AND I follow the rocky path through the dense woods filled with juniper and oak trees. When we reach the twin waterfalls, the smell of burning wood grows stronger. We follow it and find Will. He's far from the beaten path, sitting in front of a small campfire. He leans forward, squinting at us. "Noah? Carson? What are you guys doing here?"

Before either of us can answer, I hear a rustling in the woods. We stop. Footsteps draw closer. Suddenly Hawk appears right in front of us, carrying a bundle of wood and sticks. He looks like he just stepped out of *The Rocky Horror Picture Show*. "What the hell . . . ?" He glares at us like we're trespassers. "Who told you we were here?" He sees the map in my hand and snatches it. "Who drew this?"

"Um, Will's friend Quindlan," I say.

"Quindlan? *Damn* that idiot. What's he thinking?" He turns to Will.

"Hawk, dude, calm down," Will says. "Noah and Carson are cool. There's nothing to worry about."

"Oh, there's plenty to worry about. I told you, Will, I never should have given Noah that note." He gives Carson and me a disgusted look, then marches to the fire and tosses in the map. The paper flares up quickly, then dies, smoldering. Not exactly the reception I was expecting.

"Don't mind Hawk," Will says. "He overreacts to everything. Come here, sit down. I'm glad you guys found me."

As we weave our way over to Will, Hawk throws the wood into a pile, plucks a rope from the ground, pulls out a pocket knife, and cuts the rope in half. Mumbling to himself, he proceeds to tie one end of the rope to the branch of a tree.

We take seats on either side of Will. "So you guys met Quindlan and Doomsday, huh? What did you think?"

"I think they're both pretty nuts," Carson says. "Especially Doomsday. Quindlan's all right, I guess. His dog's pretty cool. Anyway, I'm glad Quindlan drew us that map. We've been worried about you."

I watch Hawk from the corner of my eye. He's tying the other end of the rope to an adjacent tree. When he's done, he plucks a wet towel from a nearby branch and hangs it on the line to dry. I look around the campsite. A jar of peanut butter and a loaf of bread sit on a tree stump. A gallon of milk is chilling in a bucket of ice. A sleeping bag is spread out on the ground. Hawk is taking care of Will. Making sure he has everything he needs. I consider asking how things went in jail, but I figure that's not a good idea.

"Will?" I say. "Quindlan told me you knew the kid they found near Town Lake. I'm really sorry."

"Yeah. Paul Mateo. I hadn't seen him in years, but he was one of the first kids I got to know in foster care after my parents died. We were both, well, different, which is why we became friends, but Paul got teased a lot. The other kids called him faggot and queer. I feel bad now because I never stood up for him. I guess I was afraid those same kids would turn on me, too. Anyway, I found out that Paul had been hustling on the streets. Right before the murder. I had no idea."

"Hustling?" I say. "You mean . . ."

"Right."

No one says anything for a while. Hawk is standing quietly by the clothesline. He's been listening the whole time.

"Hey, Will?" Carson says. "How did you find out it was Paul? I thought the police weren't releasing his name because he was under eighteen."

Will opens his mouth, but he doesn't say anything.

Meanwhile Hawk strolls over and sits opposite us. He lights a cigarette and takes a long drag. "Be careful what you say, Will," he mutters.

Hawk and Will lock eyes for a moment; Will nods, then turns to us. "The undercover detective I'd been working with, the one who had me wear the wire, he told me it was Paul Mateo who was murdered. That's one of the reasons he thought I should disappear for a while. If Warren Banks isn't the killer, then the guy's still out there. And if he is still free, he may have been following me, too. Anyway, the detective also told me that the police just hired a criminal profiler.

A guy from the FBI. They're trying to cover all their bases. The case is close to being solved. At least, that's what he tells me."

"But, Will?" I look around the campsite. "How long can you stay here? I mean, I understand about disappearing, but this place doesn't look safe to me."

"I won't be here much longer," he says. "Turns out my social worker found me a home. She says it's a good one. When things blow over, I'll move in. Plus, Hawk's been helping me out. Even lined me up with a job, waiting tables at Kerbey Lane. If everything goes well, I'll make it to L.A. right after I graduate."

I look at Hawk, wondering what kind of trouble he's in and whether he's here in the woods with Will because he's hiding out from the police. It's highly possible. "Eh, you give me too much credit, Will," Hawk says. He takes a long drag and blows a smoke ring.

"So, enough of this morbid stuff," Will says. "You guys got my note. Are you ready for Saturday night?"

"We're ready," Carson says. "Thanks for setting up the gig, Will. Really, we owe you one."

"No problem. Turned out the Red Room had an opening and the owner took my word for it that you guys were good." Will looks at me. "And now, I get to keep my promise to Noah. Remember? I'm going to help you write that song for Aubrey."

"Tonight?" I say.

"Of course. You'll need to sing it for her on Saturday. Come on." He stands up. "Do you have the book I gave you?"

"Oh . . . no. I didn't bring it."

"That's all right, I'll get mine. Hey, Hawk, keep Carson company for a while, okay? Noah and I are going to write a song."

Hawk eyes Carson and blows another smoke ring. "Sure thing."

Will leads me several yards away to a big limestone rock. We take seats atop, and Will pulls out his notebook. "Now, tell me ten things you hate about Aubrey."

"What? Ten things I *hate*? I thought this was supposed to be a love song."

"Well, in your case an *anti*-love song might work best. Especially if Aubrey needs some persuading. Words can be more powerful if you write the opposite of how you feel."

"Sorry, Will, but that doesn't make sense."

"Oh, it does. Come on, give it a try."

Will and I brainstorm, and when we're done, I have the bare bones of the strangest song I've ever written. A few lines of the chorus, too. "So if Aubrey never speaks to me again, I can blame you, right?" I say.

"After Aubrey hears the song, she'll be begging for more."

"Now, *that* I highly doubt."

"Trust me, Noah. I know what I'm talking about. I've had my heart broken a few times." Will looks at me and smiles sadly. "And I know what unrequited love is like." There's a tense silence between us. I feel my face growing hot. Suddenly I realize that my knee is touching Will's. I pull it away. "Listen, Will, I can't—"

"I know." He hangs his head. "Sorry, I shouldn't have said that. It was really stupid."

"Yeah, it was."

I'm about to hop off the rock, but Will stops me. "Noah, wait, please. God, this is so awkward. Let me explain. You see, when I first saw you on the Drag, playing guitar and singing, you reminded me of the guy I told you about—the one I was seeing. The guitarist. We were together about eight months. Our breakup was pretty rough, and I'm not even sure I'm over it yet. Anyway, the day I met you I took a chance, and when I figured out you were straight, which didn't take long, I still wanted to be your friend. I just like you. That's all."

I'm sitting on the edge of the rock. My whole body is tense. "Okay, whatever. I . . . I really need to go now."

"Yeah, sure, I understand."

Will rips the pages from the book and hands them to me. I shove them into my pocket, jump off the rock, and walk back to the campfire. Will trails behind.

"Hey, you're back," Carson says. "Hawk and I were just discussing my recipe for apricot-hash jelly. He thinks I need to add a little cayenne pepper. Give it a Cajun flavor."

When I don't laugh, Carson gives me a strange look. He peers behind me and sees Will. "So . . . did you guys write the song?"

"Yeah, some of it," I say. "Carson, it's getting late. We need to head home before it's pitch black."

Carson looks back and forth between me and Will. "Is everything . . . okay?"

"Everything's fine," I say.

Will doesn't answer. He just stands there with his hands in his pockets.

"Will? You'll be there Saturday night to hear us play, right?" Carson says.

"Um, I should be."

"You'd *better* be. Come on, dude. It's our *debut*."

Will shuffles his feet. "Yeah, well, Noah's right. You guys should head home."

Carson watches us. "Okay. Well, you be careful out here. And keep in touch." He bumps fists with Hawk, then Will, and the two of us head for the clearing.

"Noah, what happened back there?" Carson says. "Why are you acting so weird?"

"Nothing *happened*. Just leave me alone, all right?"

"You didn't even say goodbye to Will."

"Shut up. I don't feel like talking right now."

He sighs. "Fine. Whatever."

We hike in silence. It's getting darker by the second. Halfway to the entrance, we hear rustling in the trees. We both freeze, and suddenly Hawk appears in the bushes. He flips on a flashlight and hands it to me. "Thought you might need this." The beam casts shadows on his face, making his freakish appearance even more ghastly.

I swallow. "Thanks."

He nods solemnly. "Listen. Both of you. Don't come back here. It could be dangerous. Someone might follow you."

"Don't worry. We're not coming back," I say.

"Good." Slowly, he lifts one side of his shirt, revealing a holster. Tucked inside, a gun. "Believe me. Will's safe."

{eleven}

"DUDE, COME on, *jump!*"

It's Friday, and Carson is going to the movies with Kat and the King of Glory youth group tonight. He's still grounded for stealing the DPCP's Lexus Wednesday night, so the two of us are sneaking out of his second-story bedroom window. Carson has already taken the plunge. Now it's my turn. I teeter on the ledge.

"Remind me again," I say. "Why am I doing this?"

"Because you need to get out of the house, dude. You've been moping around for days, and honestly, you've been a real pain in the ass. Besides, I need a ride. Just aim for this bush. It'll break your fall."

"Break my leg's more like it."

I stare at the bush Carson is pointing to. It's an overgrown holly with red berries and spiked leaves. Besides breaking my leg, I'm going to get impaled. I take a deep breath, jump, hit the bush, and roll into the grass. A painful experience, but I'm alive, and that's good enough for Carson.

"Come on, let's go." He pulls me to my feet. "Kat's waiting for us. And you'd better not chicken out. You better ask Aubrey to our gig at the Red Room."

"Yeah, right. If I can pry her away from Brandon."

When we arrive at the theater, I see the usual zealots outside the box office, waiting to buy tickets. We're about to see the new inspirational film *Spears in the Jungle*—a true story about three American missionaries martyred by some pissed-off aborigines. Just wait till the DPCP hears about this one.

At the front of the line is Brandon. Tonight he's wearing a shirt that says *Satan Sucks*. Behind him are Aubrey and Kat. "Come on, there they are!" Carson runs to the front of the line. Like a sucker, I follow.

Brandon, Kat, and Aubrey stare at me like I have two heads. In fact, all the zealots are giving me strange looks. "Um, Noah?" Aubrey says. "You're bleeding." She taps her right cheek.

"What?" I touch my face. That damn holly bush. I turn to Carson. "Why didn't you tell me I was bleeding, you idiot?"

He shrugs. "Sorry. I didn't notice."

"Here." I shove some money into his hand. "Buy my ticket. I'm going to the bathroom."

After rinsing the blood off my face and neck, I stare at myself in the mirror. Besides having been mauled by a shrub, I'm not a bad-looking guy. And I've got a decent personality.

At least, I *think* I do. Even *guys* are attracted to me. So what does Brandon have that I don't?

Nothing.

Everything.

He's got Aubrey.

Carson doesn't even wait for me. Some friend. The guy at the door is holding my ticket. "Thanks." I snatch it from his hand and walk into the theater. The lights are dim, and since it's a low-budget Christian film, instead of previews, they're flashing church advertisements on the screen. I look around and see the youth group sitting dead center. Brandon's in the first row of zealots, looking all cozy sitting next to Aubrey. Beside Aubrey is Kat, and next to Kat is Carson. The loser didn't even save me a seat. The rest of that row is filled with more zealots. To top it off, Marty is in the row behind them, waving me over.

"Noah, dude, come on, sit over here!" As usual, Marty is trying to be all hip and cool, all relevant, all down with the teen scene. But he can't fool me. The biggest question on Marty's mind is *So, Noah, how's your walk with the Lord?*

"How've you been?" he says. "I haven't spoken to you in a while."

"Fine." I'm in no mood for Marty's small talk. Especially when I see Aubrey laughing at one of Brandon's jokes. I peer over and see their fingers loosely entwined. A knot twists in my stomach.

To keep my eyes off the lovebirds, I begin reading the church advertisements, and I see one for King of Glory. *A place where everyone is welcome.* Anger rises in my chest. I turn to Marty and blurt out, "Actually, I recently joined another church." I say this pretty loudly. It's intentional. Aubrey spins around and gives me a strange look.

"Really?" Marty says. "That's a surprise. Which one?"

"Westboro Baptist. Have you heard of it? It's pretty cool. We have these awesome Bible studies, mostly from the book of Leviticus, and then we head out for some serious gay-bashing afterward. This guy I know from King of Glory, he used to go there, but he's in jail now. Anyway, it's very intense. You should try it sometime." Heads are turning now. One of them is Brandon's.

Brandon laughs nervously. "Hey, uh, Marty . . . don't take Noah too seriously, okay? He's got one wicked sense of humor."

Carson narrows his eyes at me. "Yeah, Noah's one funny guy."

Honestly, I can't tell whether I'm pissed off at them or at myself. Maybe it's both.

I guess all the zealots have heard about their former Sunday school teacher's double life, because they're squirming in their seats. Lucky for them, the lights turn off and the movie begins. As the pagan aborigines slash their way through the jungle with huge machetes, Marty leans over and whispers in my ear, "I don't think he did it."

"What are you talking about?"

"Warren Banks. Yesterday I went to visit him in jail."

"You *visited* him?"

"Yeah. That's what pastors do, Noah. Visit people who need help. Anyway, Banks told me *his* version of what happened. He said he was with Kyle the night he was killed, but they only had a drink together and talked. After that, Kyle went off with a guy who was asking for spare change. Kyle was going to take him to an all-night diner, get him something to eat. That's the last Banks saw of Kyle Lester."

"And you believe that?"

"Well, I can't be one hundred percent sure, but he seems to be telling the truth. Plus, Banks didn't even know the other boy who was murdered—the one found by Town Lake. And the medical examiners haven't been able to determine yet if the boy was killed before or after Banks was arrested. Anyway, Banks is hiring a good lawyer. They're going to fight it."

"But what about the whole Westboro Baptist thing? Banks was a *member* of that place. Those people are *sick*. I saw them on the news."

"I know. I asked Warren about that, too. He told me he'd made a huge mistake joining that church. He'd been fighting his sexual orientation for a long time. It seems he got bad advice from this radical online support group. Warren believed if he could be repulsed enough by homosexuals, it might cure him. Obviously it didn't work."

"*Cure him?*" I shake my head. "This is unbelievable. Listen, Marty, I'm sorry, but I'm not buying that story. I think Banks is lying. I think he's guilty."

Marty shrugs. "You could be right."

I lean back in my seat, and as I watch the movie, something nags at me. Banks claimed it was a guy in need of money who was last seen with Kyle. But who?

Twenty minutes into the movie, I reach the conclusion that *Spears in the Jungle* is one of the worst films of the year.

Not only is the acting atrocious, but there's so much melodrama I want to barf. Worst of all, when the aborigines spear the missionaries, there's no blood.

Anyway, I must be one sick dude, because when the camera flashes back to the United States and everyone is at the missionaries' funeral, and the seven-year-old son one of the dead guys stands up and gives a tearful speech about how proud he is of his father because he risked his life to spread God's Word to the aborigines, I lose it and start to laugh. And once I get going, I can't stop. Carson turns around and gives me a dirty look, and that's when I see that he's been crying—which makes me crack up even more.

"Um, Noah, I think you'd better leave," Marty says. "Now."

"Yeah, I think you're right." I get up, and I notice that Aubrey is doubled over in her seat. One hand is cupped over her mouth, and her shoulders are shaking. She's laughing. A wicked surge of pleasure rises inside me. As I walk up the aisle, one of the zealots begins to clap. I turn and take a bow.

Outside the theater, I hear someone running behind me. "Noah, wait!"

It's Aubrey. "Oh . . . hey."

She's not laughing anymore. "Noah, I don't know what to say. I just . . . well, how *are* you?"

Depressed. Angry. Guilty. Losing my mind. All of the above. "I'm fine." She's not buying it. Aubrey's always been able to read me like a book. "How about you?" I say.

"Okay, I guess. It's been pretty crazy at home, though. The police have been at my house questioning my father about Warren Banks. And after that second boy was murdered, they came back. They think my father should know something, since he's the pastor of our church, but he doesn't. The whole thing's so strange. And scary."

"Yeah, I've been pretty freaked out over it too." I wish I could tell Aubrey everything. About Will. How I ruined our friendship by acting like a jackass. How he might be in danger. But I can't. Not now. "Hey, Aubrey? Marty told me he visited Warren Banks in prison. Has your father gone?"

She nods. "Just the other day. He thinks Banks is innocent too. I'm not sure why, because he won't talk to me about it."

We stand there for a while looking at each other, and a lump wells up in my throat. I miss Aubrey so much. I want to ask her to come with me now. We could drive to Kerbey Lane, order lemonade and chips with chili queso. Talk for hours. Laugh. Like we used to do. But of course I can't.

Instead, I say, "Well, I guess you'd better get back to the movie. You don't want to miss the exciting part. You know, when they shish-kebab the missionaries. I heard that was the plot twist. Pretty cool, huh? The aborigines are cannibals."

She gives me a wry smile. "Yeah, you're right, Noah. I better go."

"Aubrey?"

"Yeah?"

"A lot of things have happened lately. Things I can't go into right now. And, well, I know you're busy with Brandon and all, but Carson and I have a gig at this place called the Red Room. It's an underground club on Seventh and

Neches. This guy I know, Will, he set it up for us. Anyway, it's a long story, but I was wondering if you might want to hear us play. The show's next Saturday. Ten o'clock."

She nods slowly. "Sure, I'd love to come."

I realize I've been holding my breath. I let it out. "Great. Thanks. I'll see you then."

{twelve}

"HEY, NOAH, what do you think of a punk-slash-emo version of 'Amazing Grace'?"

Carson and I have been practicing for our gig all week, and I'm seriously about to lose it. After seeing *Spears in the Jungle*, he had this major conversion experience—prayed with Marty and everything—and now he wants to be baptized. "You know what I think?" I set down my guitar and hold up a hand, measuring one inch between my forefinger and thumb. "I think I'm *this close* to marching into the DPCP's bedroom and telling him what you've been up to."

Carson's eyes grow wide. "Dude, you wouldn't."

"Oh, yes I would. Now, enough of this punk hymnal crap. You need to get to work on 'Flesh-Eating Zombies.' We've got our first real show in two days, and right now, your lyrics still suck, and the music's not that great either."

I pick up my guitar and start plucking the melody of my

anti-love song for Aubrey. I've finished writing the lyrics, but I'm having serious doubts about their potential effectiveness.

I glance at Carson. He's slumped over his guitar, and there's a hurt look on his face. "Hey, listen, I'm sorry. Really, man. I shouldn't have said that. And if you want to do a punk-emo, whatever, version of 'Amazing Grace,' fine. I mean, just because it's not my thing doesn't mean it's not yours."

"Hey, Noah? What's been eating you lately? Ever since we came back from the greenbelt, you've been on edge. Something happened between you and Will. When you guys were writing that song for Aubrey. I know it."

I chew the inside of my cheek.

"Did Will make a pass at you?"

"Shut up."

"Come on, I'm joking. Look, Noah. It's not a crime to feel weirded out if a guy's into you. It's a normal reaction. What matters is what you do with it. Plus, with the way you've been brought up, it's not a surprise that you're having a hard time."

I glare at Carson. "I already told you I don't believe any of that shit."

"Well, maybe you're not as tolerant as you thought."

"Oh yeah? Let me ask *you* something, Mr. Holy Roller. Why are you so gung ho about the church scene when you know damn well their stance on gay people? They're all going to hell, didn't you know?"

"Not according to Marty."

"Oh? Have you asked him about it? Because I guarantee—"

"Yes. I have asked him. In fact, we had a long conversation about it. He told me that he's struggled with that teaching for a long time, and personally doesn't agree with it. And he doesn't think gays should try to be straight either. But he said change has to come from inside the church, and he thinks the youth group can be a catalyst."

"A catalyst? Right. I'll believe it when I see it."

"Noah? Why do you hate Marty and the youth group so much? I mean, they're really nice. At least, they are to me."

I sit there for a while. There's a brick in my stomach. "I don't hate them, Carson. It's just, well, it ticks me off how they think there's only one way to God—*their way*. I just don't buy that. I never have. My parents tried to brainwash me with that crap from birth. The thing they don't get is I have a mind of my own, and I intend to use it."

"Yeah, I understand what you mean. But the youth group's different from church. Marty's way cooler than Pastor Simpson, and way more open-minded. And it's hard to explain, but ever since that night I prayed with Marty, I feel so much better. Like . . . happy. And maybe this sounds lame, but *free*, too."

"Hmmm, maybe it's all those sins you repented from—drunkenness, rebellion, witchcraft—"

"Come on, Noah, I'm serious! I'm not cut out to be an atheist. I *like* believing in God."

"All right, fine. Believe in God. But let me ask you something. And be honest. Does this *conversion* have anything to do with Kat? More specifically, the possibility of getting into her pants?"

Carson looks up at the ceiling. "Well, I have to admit, that would be a perk and all, but—"

"See? I'm telling you, man, enjoy the good vibes now, because pretty soon Marty's gonna break the news: no sex before marriage."

"Yeah, I kind of figured that. But I was thinking, what if I have sex with Kat, then repent, then maybe do it again and repent? I mean, that could work, right?"

"You're pathetic."

"I know, I know. Anyway, I suppose I *could* wait. It would be rough, but the truth is I care about Kat. A lot. I've never felt this way about a girl before. And I like being with Marty and the youth group."

I sigh. "Whatever turns you on, man."

"Noah? Tell me the truth. What happened between you and Will?"

"Nothing *happened*. Drop it, dude."

"You acted like a jerk, didn't you?"

"Will said some things that freaked me out. I didn't know how to react. So, yeah, I acted like a jerk. Gave him the brush-off. I've been feeling guilty about it all week. Are you happy now?"

Carson nods. "I figured it was something like that. Listen, Noah, don't beat yourself up over it, all right? Besides, we'll see Will Saturday night at the Red Room. You'll work it out."

"I hope so. I just thought I was different, you know? Thought I could handle anything. Truth is, I was an asshole. I really let him down."

"Hey, it happens to everyone. Come on, let's get to work. We've got some songs to practice."

† † †

Friday afternoon, Hawk walks into ISS, hands Mr. Briggs another referral note, and takes a seat behind me. A few seconds later he taps me on the shoulder and passes me a note.

Sorry, Noah. My bad.

Hope things are cool now. Hope we can be friends.

I moved into my new home yesterday—so far so good.

See you tomorrow night. I'll be there.

Blow Aubrey away.

Will

When I turn around, Hawk has once again vanished.

{thirteen}

"**TESTING . . . ONE,** two, three. Testing . . ."

While Carson messes with the PA system, I grab my guitar, take a seat onstage, and watch people mill about the Red Room. The place is kind of a dump—broken floor planks, dirty windows, Christmas lights strung across the rafters— but I like it. We're the second of two bands tonight, which is lucky, because most of the audience from the first set is hanging around to hear us play. Will was right. The Red Room definitely draws an alternative crowd, and even though I'm not 100 percent comfortable, I'm doing all right. I'm trying.

While I'm fingering the notes to "Devil Inside My Head," Carson leans over and says, "Hey, Noah, look over there. It's Quindlan."

I look up. Quindlan smiles and waves. "Hold on, I'll be right back." I hop off the stage and weave through the crowd. "Quindlan, hey, I'm glad you're here. Have you seen Will?"

"Not yet. He stopped by the Drag this afternoon. Asked me and Doomsday to come tonight, but Dooms won't set foot in this venue. Too many pagans, I guess. Anyway, Will should be here soon. He told me he had to run back to the greenbelt. He accidentally left his book there—you know, the one he writes poetry in."

"Noah! We're on in five minutes," Carson calls.

"I'd better go. But do me a favor? Keep an eye out for Will. Tell him I need to talk to him after the show."

Back onstage, Carson and I recheck the PA system, and even though my guitar is perfectly tuned, I tweak the strings one last time. I scan the room for Aubrey and finally spot her walking through the back door. Kat follows, and behind her are Brandon and Marty. Great. Aubrey holds out her hand while the bouncer whips out a felt pen and scrawls an X on it.

"Oh, good, there they are." Carson waves. "Hi, Kat!" He turns to me. "Hey, Noah, I invited Marty and Brandon, too. I hope you don't mind."

I give Carson an icy glare. "Mind? Why would I mind?"

He sighs. "Sorry, dude. I just need a little support when I sing 'Amazing Grace.' Plus, isn't this what we want? King of Glory members hanging out in a gay club? I told you Marty was open-minded."

"Whatever." I look at Aubrey, and my stomach plummets.

"Noah?" Carson reaches over and puts a hand on my shoulder. "Let's forget everything and have a great time tonight. Just think about the music. How much we love it. That's all."

"Yeah, I guess." I close my eyes and take a deep breath. "Come on, it's time," I say. "Let's do it." We take our places at the mikes. The room is packed.

"Hey, everyone! Thanks for making it out to the Red Room tonight!" Carson yells. The crowd whistles and cheers, which gets my adrenaline flowing. We begin with the Kinks' "You Really Got Me." I wanted to play it for Will—I know he'd get a kick out of it—but he's still not here. Even so, the song turns out to be a great opening number. We've got the crowd's attention. They're all moving their heads to the beat and singing along. After that, Carson rocks out with "Flesh-Eating Zombies," which doesn't sound half bad, and next I play "Devil Inside My Head."

We do a few more songs that Carson and I wrote together. Our voices are on tonight, and the harmonies sound sweet. The crowd even digs Carson's version of "Amazing Grace." One guy shouts, "Hallelujah!" and another one chimes in, "Amen!"

Then it's my turn to go solo. I take one last look around the room. Still no Will. "Um, hi, everyone. I'm Noah. I'd like to do a song that I finished writing just a few days ago. It's for a girl I know."

Suddenly the room becomes deathly quiet. I can't even bear to glance in Aubrey's direction. I take a deep breath, play the intro, blow a few bars on the harmonica, and sing.

"I really hate your face,
Hate you were my friend in the first place,
Now there's nothing left to do,
But sing this anti-love song to you.

"You pressed me up against that tree,
in the woods—crucified me,
Kissed me, but never said you'd be
There for me,
Can't you see

"That you're sanctified, justified, glorified,
and I'm cyanide?
But that's fine, you see, fine with me.

"Did God save your soul?
Did he make you whole?
Did he set you free?
When someone else replaced me?

"Horrified of all the lies
you tell through your eyes,
But that's fine, you see, fine with me.

"I really hate your face,
Hate you were my friend in the first place,
Now there's nothing left to do,
But sing this anti-love song to you."

I hum the last few bars on my harmonica, and when I open my eyes, Aubrey is standing in the front row. While the crowd applauds—and I must say, they really *do* dig my song—she marches onto the stage, looks me in the eye, and says, "You *asshole!*"

Before I can explain to her the cryptic nature of my

lyrics, and how words are more powerful if you write the opposite of what you feel, she slaps me across the face. Hard.

I look at Carson. My left ear is buzzing.

At first he's not sure what to do, but soon a grin spreads across his face. He raises one fist in the air and shouts, "Whoa! How's *that* for rock and roll?" The crowd goes wild.

I watch Aubrey push her way toward the door. Brandon and Marty follow her, but Kat stays put.

"Jeez, I wasn't expecting that," I say. "Anyway, thanks for saving my butt, dude."

"Anytime."

At the end of the show, we take our last bows and pack up our guitars. Except for Aubrey's slap, everything went better than expected, so I guess I can't complain. I just wish Will had come. I wonder if he changed his mind at the last minute because he didn't want to face me.

"Hey, Noah?" Carson says. "Kat's giving me a ride home, okay? Are you all right without me?"

"Sure, man. I've got my car. Go for it."

I watch as the two of them stroll happily out the door. The club is empty now. I take one last look around, then climb the narrow, winding staircase to the street. Outside, Quindlan is waiting. "Hmmm, not too much damage," he says, studying the left side of my face. "She's pretty. What's her name?"

"Aubrey. She hates me now. Thinks I'm an asshole."

"Nah, I doubt it. Just wait. She'll come around."

"Will helped me write that song," I say. "And he didn't show up to hear me play it. I'm bummed."

"I don't know what happened," Quindlan says. "He said he'd be here. It's not like him."

I look up and down the street, hoping for a sign of Will. Nothing. "It's probably my fault," I say. "Last time I saw him I acted like a jerk. Anyway, maybe we should go to the campsite and look for him? I've got my car, I can drive."

"No, not tonight, Noah. It's pitch black out there. Even with a flashlight, we'd never find our way. Besides, Will left for the campsite hours ago. He could be anywhere by now. My guess is he's home, safe and sound."

"Yeah. I heard he liked his new foster home."

Suddenly I hear a dog barking. Hercules turns the corner and runs to Quindlan. "Hercules, hey, bud," Quindlan says. As he stoops down to pet him, Doomsday appears. "Hey, Dooms, show's over," Quindlan says. "Thanks for watching Hercules. You should have heard Noah play. He was awesome."

Doomsday gazes at the neon sign in the window of the Red Room. He shakes his head and looks at me. "'Broad is the road that leads to destruction and many enter through it. But narrow is the road to life . . .'" He pauses, waiting for me to finish the verse.

"'And few find it,'" I say. "Matthew seven, verses thirteen and fourteen."

Quindlan sighs. "Come on, Dooms, give the kid a break. It's late, Noah. You should go home. And don't worry, if I run into Will, I'll be sure to give him hell for missing your show."

{fourteen}

I WAKE up with a jolt. I'm out of breath, covered in sweat. My hands and feet are freezing. The left side of my face hurts. For hours I've been running through the woods along the path leading to Will's hideout in the greenbelt. But none of that makes sense, because here I am, safe in bed. All a dream.

I turn over and peer at my alarm clock. It's five a.m. Everything starts coming back now—the show, Aubrey, my song, the slap. Carson ditching me for Kat. Quindlan and Doomsday outside the Red Room. Will never showing up.

Last night it was too dark to search for Will. But it's morning now, and the sun will be up soon. I feel dread in the pit of my stomach.

I get up and dress in the clothes lying in a heap by the side of my bed. I stuff my cell phone into my pocket—just in case—and grab the car keys from the kitchen counter.

By the time I reach the entrance to the greenbelt, there's just enough light to see along the rocky path. I run until I come to the twin waterfalls. I weave through the brush. Will's there, just like I feared he'd be. Facedown. Dead.

† † †

"So, tell me again," Officer Frank says. "Will was supposed to meet you last night for a show?"

"Yes, that's right." The police arrived fifteen minutes after I called 911. Officer Frank and I are standing under a juniper tree. I watch an investigator snap photos of Will. The killer's note and the rope used to strangle Will have been marked off with numbers. The investigator snaps photos of them, too. Two other officers have already cordoned off a large area with yellow tape and flagged a path to the body.

"And the last time you heard from Will was Friday afternoon at school?" he goes on.

"Yeah. Will's friend gave me a note from him. In it, he said he'd be at the gig. Didn't I tell you this already?" My head aches and a deep tiredness has settled between my shoulder blades. I want to go home and sleep, and when I wake up, maybe all of *this* will be a dream.

While Officer Frank jots down a few notes in his book, another investigator, the guy who's been lifting footprints, walks over to us. "So, you're Noah? The boy who called 911?"

"Yes."

"I'm Detective Robinson. I need to know what happened before the police came. Did you touch anything, move the body, tamper with any potential evidence?"

"Um . . ." A lump rises in my throat; my heart pounds. I shove my hands into my pockets and run a finger across the edge of Will's book, which was tossed not far from his body. "No. I mean . . . well, yes. When I saw Will on the ground, I ran over to him. He used to camp out here, and I thought he might have been sleeping or hurt. I rolled him over and that's when I realized what happened. I saw the bruises on his neck, the blood on his shirt, and the note under the rock. The rope, too. I lifted his shirt and saw the cross. That's when I threw up. I didn't mess with anything, though. Right away I grabbed my phone and dialed. The police showed up maybe fifteen minutes later." When I'm done speaking, I realize that my armpits are soaked with sweat.

Detective Robinson studies me for a while. His expression isn't friendly. "Is there anything else you want to tell us, Noah? Anything at all?"

You mean that I never got to say I was sorry? I clutch Will's book tighter. I feel anger rising inside my chest. "Yeah, actually there is. I thought the killer was in jail. I thought this wouldn't happen again. But it did. Obviously you've got the wrong guy. Obviously the police aren't doing their job."

"Whoa, son," Detective Robinson says. "You're jumping the gun here. There are a lot of facts you don't know."

Officer Frank puts a hand on my shoulder. "You've been through a lot, Noah. Please try to stay calm. And believe me, we're doing everything we can. The medical examiner should be here any minute. And the local police and the FBI have been working together. We're going to solve the case. It's very complicated. What Detective Robinson said is true. We don't have all the facts yet. We will soon."

The photographer walks over and, without asking, snaps several photos of me. I want to rip the camera out of his hands. My face burns. I feel naked, exposed.

Then, from the corner of my eye, I see movement in the bushes. Suddenly Quindlan appears. He runs, jumps the crime scene tape, and races over to Will. I look around, expecting the police to tackle him, do something, but instead, they just watch.

Quindlan kneels beside Will. Detective Robinson calls out, "Please, be careful! Don't disturb anything!"

I watch as Quindlan covers his face with his hands. He moans, picks up a rock, flings it into the woods, and screams, "Damn it!"

"I said, don't disturb anything!"

Quindlan turns around. "Shut up! I knew this kid! All right!"

Everyone's silent. I can't figure out what's going on. Why are they letting Quindlan, of all people, near Will's body?

Quindlan scans the small crowd of police, investigators, and forensic workers. When he sees me standing next to Officer Frank, his eyes widen and he quickly turns away.

"Noah, I have to call your parents now," Officer Frank says. "They need to know what's going on. Please, give me the number. I'll take you to the police station. They can meet you there."

"Wait," I say, motioning to Quindlan. "Who is he?"

"Sorry, I can't tell you that, son. We need to go. Now."

† † †

My father meets me at the police station. He's pretty up-set. "Noah, why didn't you tell Mom and me what was going on? You could have gotten hurt. For heaven's sake, *killed*. You should *not* have gone out to the woods by yourself."

I can barely look at him. "Sorry." My voice is flat.

"Sorry? Do you have any idea what you've put us through?"

What I want to say is *Do you have any idea what I've been through, Dad? Or do you not really care because Will was gay?* But instead, I mumble, "No, I guess not." It's the most I've said to him all week.

My father calls my mother, who apparently is too hyster-ical to appear at the station, and tells her I'm okay. Then Of-ficer Frank leads us to a room, sits us down, and asks me a bunch of questions. How long have I known Will? How did we meet? How did I know he was in the woods? My mind is a blur, but I answer everything as well as I can.

"Mr. Nordstrom," Officer Frank says, "I need to ask Noah a few personal questions, and for the sake of the in-vestigation, it's best if you're not present."

My father looks back and forth between Officer Frank and me. "Well, I'm not sure. Noah? How do you feel about me not being here?"

"It's all right, Dad."

"Do I need a lawyer?" my father says. "I mean, Noah's not a suspect, is he?"

"No, no, nothing like that, Mr. Nordstrom. It should only take about ten minutes. I'll call you when we're done."

My father nods, gets up, and walks out of the room.

Officer Frank clears his throat. "Noah, I asked your fa-ther to leave because this can be a difficult subject between fathers and sons. Also, I'm aware of your father's occupation and conservative beliefs, and I know he may not approve of your answers. We have to cover all angles in the case. As you know, this murder appears to be another gay hate crime. We're aware of Will's sexual orientation, so I need to understand your relationship with him. Were you and Will friends or . . . more than friends?"

"Friends," I say, feeling the stab of guilt return.

"Okay." He jots something down in his book. "And are you gay or straight?"

"Straight. But why does that matter?"

"Well, so far, the killer seems to be targeting gay teenagers who have been in the foster care system. Like I said, we're covering all angles. I don't believe you're in danger, Noah, but if your relationship with Will had been intimate, I would have strongly urged you to take precautions. Even though it wasn't, you should be very careful. We just don't know what this killer will do next."

I think about this for a moment. "Officer Frank, I need to ask you something. It's important."

"Okay."

"The man at the greenbelt, the one who jumped the crime scene tape, I know him. His name's Quindlan. He was a friend of Will's—a homeless guy who hangs out on the Drag. Why didn't anyone stop him back there?"

Officer Frank sighs. "I'm sorry, Noah. I'm not at liberty to tell you. And please don't worry about it. I'm going to call your father now. Just go home and get some rest. You've been through a severe trauma, and you've seen horrific things, things a boy your age shouldn't see, and it'll take time to readjust." He hands me his card. "Call me if you remember anything else. Or if you just need to talk. I'll be here. Of course, your privacy will be protected, but expect a lot of coverage of the murder on the news. Will's autopsy results and the forensic testing will be in by next week. Hopefully, we'll have some answers and a few more leads by then."

My father wants to take me right home, but I insist on retrieving the van parked by the greenbelt. "Noah, are you *sure* you want to drive home? Mom and I can come back later and pick up the van. It's not a problem."

"I can drive, Dad. It's not like I'm hurt. I'll be fine."

He argues awhile longer, but when he realizes I'm not changing my mind, he finally gives up. "All right, then. Let's go."

I get into his car, and he drives me to the greenbelt. We're silent the whole way. I'm relieved my father doesn't ask questions about my private conversation with Officer Frank.

The entrance to the hiking trail is barricaded, and police are standing guard. "Noah, I know we have a lot of unresolved issues and we need to talk, but—"

"No," I say. "There's really nothing to talk about, Dad."

He lowers his head and sighs. "I'm truly sorry about Will. I can only imagine how difficult this is for you. Mom and I, we're just concerned for your safety. I hope you can understand."

"Whatever, Dad." I open the door.

"Noah, wait. Why don't you follow me? I'd feel better if you were in my rearview."

"Dad. Please go. It's a ten-minute drive. I said I'm fine."

He waits while I get into my van. I start up the engine and wave him on. Reluctantly, he drives off. When I see him turn the corner, a surge of anger floods through me. My whole body tenses, and I punch the steering wheel over and over. When I'm finally done, I look up and see Quindlan walking down the street.

I shut off the engine and bolt out of the van. "Hey! Quindlan! Wait up!"

He turns, sees me, and continues walking.

"I said *wait*!" I run after him. When I catch up, I say, "I want to know what's going on. Who *are* you?"

He glances around nervously. "Don't draw any attention, just follow me."

He leads me down a path into the woods. After a quarter mile or so, he stops, turns around, and whispers, "The best thing to do is pretend you never met me."

"What? No. I won't do that. Besides, I think I figured it out. You're an undercover detective, aren't you? In fact, you're the one who had Will wear the wire. You're the one who *used* him. Took what you wanted and tossed him aside. You knew he was in danger, you knew he was a target, but you did nothing to protect him. And now he's *dead*."

"Noah, please, there are a lot of things you don't understand."

"Oh, I understand. Everything you told me was a lie. You should have been there for Will, protecting him. I thought you were his friend, but it turns out—"

"Look, Noah, you're not the only person who lost a friend today. Now, what you said is true. I take full responsibility for what happened. I thought Will was safe. I even helped him find a new home. He was happy there. Supposedly the killer was in jail. It was my mistake, my blunder.

And now I have to live with it. In fact, right now I have to go back to the Drag and break the news to Doomsday."

"And who *is* Doomsday?"

"Exactly who you think he is. A homeless man with a tragic story. And he's a friend of mine too. In my line of work, it's hard not to get close to the people you infiltrate."

"Infiltrate?"

"Yeah, I know it's a cold word, but it's the truth."

"What about Will's friend Hawk? Do you know him too?"

He nods slowly. "I do. I know he helped Will out from time to time, but I don't trust him. He's bad news, Noah. Trouble. Keep your distance."

I think about Hawk's gun. The way he protected Will out in the woods. Sure, maybe that was illegal, but it's more than Quindlan did. Certainly more than I did.

"Okay, I've got one more question. All that stuff you told me about your father being a hard-core evangelical, working with gang members in the South Bronx—was that true, or were you just *infiltrating*?"

He sighs. "I wish it wasn't true, but it is. I left home after my brother committed suicide. Put myself through school and became a detective. I lost my brother, and now I've lost Will. So, yeah, I do understand how you feel, Noah. More than you realize. But now do yourself a favor. Go home. Try to make things right with your dad. Try your best to forget . . ." Tears well up in his eyes. He looks away. "Everything."

"But I can't forget. I screwed up too. Last time I saw Will I was an ass to him. I wanted to apologize, and I never got to."

"Noah, look, I understand, but that's water under the bridge now. You need to let it go."

"Will there be a funeral? After the autopsy?"

"A funeral?" Quindlan shakes his head. "No. I expect the media will cover the story closely, which is a good thing. These hate crimes need to be exposed, and we need to find the killer, but as for a funeral, who would come? Who would pay for it? Who would even *care*? Will had no family. He dealt drugs. Got arrested. In the end, he was murdered because he was easy prey—a gay foster kid. When the media moves on to their next story, Will won't even be dead. He'll just be one of the less-dead."

"The less-dead?"

"It's a term we use. Think about it, Noah. If someone like, say, *you* were murdered, it would be this big huge deal, because you have a family and there are tons of people who care about you. But if you're someone like Kyle, Paul, or Will—homeless, no family, in trouble with the law— well, when you're dead, you're really less-dead. Do you understand?"

"Yeah, I do."

Quindlan reaches into his pocket and takes out a pen and paper. He scribbles something down and hands it to me. "I need to keep my cover. I'm in the middle of a narcotics investigation, and I shouldn't be doing this, but I figure I can trust you. Just remember, Noah: I'm a homeless guy who hangs out on the Drag with a crazy street evangelist. Nothing more."

{fifteen}

MY ROOM smells like Limburger cheese. At least, that's what Melanie tells me every time she walks in. Mainly it's because I haven't showered in four days, but there's also that half-eaten gyro I shoved under my bed a couple of nights ago, along with a slice of pizza and a carton of moo shu pork. Carson's been bringing all my favorite foods, but I have no appetite.

Atop my desk, the TV is droning. I've been watching local news round the clock. Right now a man from the Austin GLBT group is being interviewed. "Yes, we're very concerned," he says. "For years Austin has been a safe haven for gays and lesbians in the state of Texas, and now we're living in fear. . . ."

Newspapers are stacked on my dresser. Articles about each murder. Questions about Warren Banks and the Westboro church. Is one person responsible for the killings or is there a hate group involved? The police claim they have things under control. The FBI is continuing a thorough investigation. It's just a matter of time before they make another arrest.

There's a knock at my door. "Noah? Can I come in?" It's Melanie. She just got home from school—a place I haven't been in a while.

I roll from my stomach to my back. "Yeah, whatever, come on in, Mel."

She sits on my bed and crinkles her nose. "Noah, there's an oil slick on your pillow. That's *gross*."

"Yeah? Maybe I like oil slicks. Maybe I like gross. Maybe I like Limburger cheese, too."

"Come on, this isn't funny! You need to get out of bed!"

That's what my parents have been telling me for the past few days. My mother even begged me to see this shrink who goes to our church—supposedly he uses biblical principals when he psychoanalyzes you—but I flat-out refused. Screw talking. Especially to a church member. I just want to be left alone.

Melanie shakes me. I pull the covers over my head and will her to disappear. Finally she stops. The room is quiet again. For some reason, my yeasty smell is comforting. Who knows, maybe if I lie here long enough, I'll rise like a loaf of bread. Just as I'm about to doze off, I hear "Noah? Whose book is this?"

Suddenly I remember I left Will's notebook of poems on my dresser. I lift off the covers and sit up. Melanie's thumbing through the pages. I snatch it from her. "Mel. Get out of here. I'm trying to sleep."

"I asked, whose book is it!"

"It's mine, all right? Now get lost."

"You think I'm stupid? It's not *yours*. I know what your handwriting looks like. Besides, those poems are good." She scrunches up her nose again. "Yours *suck*."

"Gee thanks."

"Plus there are some weird things written in the margins. Things that don't make sense."

"What do you mean?"

She rolls her eyes. "I thought it was your book, Noah. Don't you know what's inside of it?"

The truth is I don't. Every time I pick up Will's book, I think about the one he gave to me. The one I tossed into the trash.

"It's *his* book, isn't it?" Melanie asks. "Will's?"

The kid's way too smart for her own good. And since I'm too tired to argue, I nod. "Yeah."

"I can tell. The handwriting's the same as on that note he left you, remember? The night we played baseball in the backyard?" She pauses. "You liked him a lot, didn't you?"

"Yeah. I did."

"Me too. He was nice. And I'm sorry, Noah. Your poems don't suck. They're good too. Really good."

"Thanks, Mel." I open Will's book to make sure Quindlan's note is still inside. It is. I read the words *Just in case*. Just in case what? Below that is Quindlan's cell phone number. I don't plan to call him, but the seven digits are already stored in my brain, whether I like it or not.

"Melanie? Listen, this is important. You can't tell anyone about this book. Not Mom, not Dad. No one."

"All right. But why?"

"Well . . . because Will didn't give it to me. I sort of took it. When I found Will, you know, dead, in the woods, I saw the book lying in a pile of leaves. Before the police came, I stuffed it into my pocket."

"Oh. You mean you weren't supposed to do that?"

"Right. It's sort of like stealing. Even though I know Will would have wanted me to have it. Anyway, I could get into *a lot* of trouble if anyone found out."

Melanie's eyes get all wide and teary. "You mean they could send you away, to the farm?"

I really hate doing this to Mel, but I don't have much of a choice. "It's a possibility."

"I won't tell anyone, Noah. I promise."

Melanie and I play three games of Uno, and when she finally leaves to do her homework, I prop up my pillow, lie back, and open Will's book. I've been avoiding it long enough; I figure it's time. First I skim through the pages. On them is a collection of poems and songs—some original, some not—along with Will's scattered thoughts. Interspersed are quotes from famous authors and musicians. Some of the entries are dated. The first one reads:

May 15th
A Swim in Barton Springs
I'm the algae, skimming the surface,
airy and green, just above the deep sadness
down below, always threatening.

This is a side of Will I didn't know. If he was depressed, he didn't show it. I wish I had paid more attention. I wish I'd been a better friend.

I read the next few entries, and each one is more haunting than the one before. I'm about to put the book away, but then I think of something. The day Will and I met. Three Saturdays ago. I count on my fingers. October ninth. I find the page, and there it is. My Lead Belly song.

My girl, my girl, don't lie to me.
Tell me, where did you sleep last night?
In the pines, in the pines, where the sun don't ever shine,
I would shiver the whole night through.

I stare at the words for a long time, remembering what Will said to me that day. *Man, someone must have seriously broken your heart.* How did he know? And why didn't I realize what he was really saying? His heart was broken too. Sure, I couldn't be with Will *that way*, but why did I have to let him down? I run my fingers over the words. A lump swells in my throat, and finally, for the first time since I saw Will dead in the woods, I begin to cry. And once I start, it's hard to stop. After a while, I grab a wad of tissues and blow my nose. That's when I notice something written in the margin, just like Melanie said. It's a poem of sorts, followed by a Bible passage and a string of numbers in no particular order. She's right. It doesn't make sense. And the handwriting is different too. Shaky. Like when I broke my right arm in sixth grade and had to learn to write with my left hand.

Potter's Field
Field of blood where they bury the stillborn,
the unclaimed, the forgotten.
Those with no voice, and no name.
John 8
5554371

I grab my Bible from the shelf, blow off the dust, and look up John, chapter eight. Weird. It's the story of the woman caught in adultery. I've heard it many times before. Basically it goes like this: The religious leaders brought a woman to Jesus and said, "We found her in bed with a man who's not her husband. According to the Law of Moses, she should be stoned. What do *you* say?" But Jesus didn't answer them. Instead, he knelt down and drew in the sand with his finger. When they continued to press him for an answer, he stood up and said, "If any of you is without sin, let him throw the first stone."

While I sit there trying to make sense of it all, Carson knocks on my door. I slip Will's book under the covers. "Dude, you're reading your Bible! Are you having a change of heart?" Carson says.

"Please. Stop," I say.

"All right, but look what I brought you this time." Carson holds up a brown paper bag and pulls out a pint of Ben & Jerry's Cherry Garcia. He pops the lid and waves it under my nose. "Come on, you know you can't resist."

Surprisingly, my stomach begins to growl. He hands me the ice cream along with a spoon and takes a seat on my bed. I shovel a few spoonfuls into my mouth. The fat seeps into my veins. "Mmm, this is good. Thanks, man."

He nods. "Anytime. Listen, Noah, I can't stay long—the DPCP's got me on a leash—but, well, here." Carson reaches into his pocket and hands me a piece of paper. "I saw Hawk in school today and he gave me this note. All he said was 'Make sure Noah sees it.'"

I swallow hard, set down the carton of ice cream, and unfold the paper.

Austin Memorial Cemetery
Burial for Will Reed
Saturday, 11 a.m.

Burial? I think about the poem I just read. Bizarre. "So, I guess they're done with the autopsy," I say. "I guess it's all over."

"Yeah, looks that way. Hey, listen, dude, I'm really sorry, but I can't go to the burial with you. I wish I could, but I got a job. At Guitar Center. I start Saturday. I'll be on the floor, helping people try out instruments. It's not Kinkos, but the DPCP's really jazzed about it. Now, I know it's taking time away from band practice, but I figure I can network with the employees, maybe even the customers, set us up with a few more gigs in town. What do you think?"

I'm barely listening. Carson peers at me. "Noah? Hey, are you okay?"

"Oh . . . yeah. I'm fine. Hey, that's great, about the job. Congratulations, man."

"Thanks. So, are you going to the burial? Because, I was thinking, it might help. You know, bring some closure, or whatever they call it."

"Yeah. I'll go."

"Good. And, Noah? I know this has been rough, but you need to forgive yourself. You're gonna drive yourself crazy if you don't."

"I know." I look down, run my hand along the outline of Will's book hidden beneath the covers.

"Okay, well, I'd better run," Carson says. "There's a youth group meeting tonight. My mom invited Kat for dinner, and I'm supposed to make the salad. I just hope the DPCP behaves himself." At the mention of Kat, I immediately think of Aubrey, and the ache inside my chest returns in full force.

"Carson? Does Aubrey know it was me who found Will's body?"

"She knows. I told her."

This makes me feel even worse. Aubrey knows, and she hasn't bothered to come see me. She hasn't even called. "I guess she's still pissed about the song?"

"Ah, don't worry about it. She'll come around." Carson picks up the ice cream and hands it to me. "Noah? Remember Maslow's hierarchy of needs. Food comes before girls. You need to eat."

I take another bite. "Okay."

"So, you think you might come to school tomorrow?"

I shrug. "I may give it a shot."

"Cool." He holds out his fist. I press mine against it. "But take my advice, okay? Shower. Because if you walk into the

Rock smelling like that, you could be charged with assault with a deadly weapon."

I give Carson the finger. He grins. "That's more like it."

When Carson leaves, I pull out Will's book and reread the poem in the margin. *Potter's Field. Field of Blood.* I stare at the string of numbers written below. On a whim, I grab my cell phone and dial. After two rings, a woman picks up. "Austin Memorial Cemetery, may I help you?"

{sixteen}

HERE'S WHAT I figure out on the way to the cemetery: Dead people get funerals. The less-dead, if they're lucky, get a hole in the ground.

It's the first really cold day of autumn, and the wind is whipping across the field of tombstones. I climb a grassy hill. In the distance I see Quindlan, Doomsday, and Hawk gathered near Will's grave site. There's a chaplain, too, wearing a collar and holding a Bible. Bouquets of flowers dot the landscape, but the place I'm headed for is barren.

Hawk leaves the others and walks over to me. "Noah, hey. You got my note."

"Yeah. Thanks for letting me know about this."

"No problem. I thought you'd want to be here. When I heard it was a sixteen-year-old kid who found Will's body at the greenbelt, I figured it was you. You and Carson were the only ones who knew about the place. And when you didn't show up at school the next few days, it was pretty obvious. Anyway, are you okay?"

"No, I'm not."

"Me neither. I still can't believe what happened. None of it makes sense. Will was supposed to meet you that night, hear you play, then go home to his new place. He liked it there. I thought he was all right. I keep blaming myself, like I should have done more. But what? I've been running it through my head, trying to make sense of it. I just don't know why he went back to the campsite."

"I do," I say. "He went to get his book of poems. He'd accidentally left it there."

"How do you know that?"

"Quindlan told me. He was at the Red Room the night Carson and I played. He'd seen Will earlier that day. Will told him he'd lost his book and was going back to the greenbelt to find it."

Hawk turns and glances at Quindlan. For a brief moment their eyes meet. Hawk looks away. "Noah? Did Quindlan tell you anything else? Anything about me?"

I hesitate. "No, nothing." It's a lie, of course. I remember Quindlan's exact words: *He's bad news, Noah. Trouble. Keep your distance.* And now I realize that Hawk wasn't at the Red Room either.

"What about Doomsday?" Hawk says. "Was he there the night you played?"

"Yeah. I mean, no. He came later on, when our gig was over. The Red Room caters to a gay crowd, and apparently Doomsday didn't approve of the venue.

Hawk nods slowly. "Interesting."

I wonder if Hawk knows that Quindlan's an undercover cop. I'm dying to ask, but it's too risky. Instead, I say, "So, you know Quindlan and Doomsday pretty well, then?"

"Let's just say I know them well enough. But, Noah, we better go. They're about to start."

Hawk and I take our places around the burial plot. I nod hello to Quindlan, Doomsday, and the chaplain and then peer into the rectangular hole dug in the ground. Inside is a simple pinewood casket. Nearby, a concrete slab is lying on its side. It reads:

WILL REED
1993–2010

Seventeen years. Over just like that. Reading those dates feels like being punched in the stomach. I think about Will's plans for next year. California. A job. Helping kids like him—alone and gay—find peace with who they are.

"Shall we begin?" the chaplain says. He clears his throat and takes out a sheet of paper. His script. "We're gathered here today to bury our dear friend Will Reed, a young boy whose life was taken suddenly and unexpectedly. As some of you know, Will loved poetry." I have to admit, the chaplain's acting skills are pretty polished. He obviously never met Will, but you'd think they were long-lost friends.

I glance at Quindlan and wonder if he supplied the chaplain with the notes.

"One of Will's favorite poems," the chaplain continues, "was 'The Road Not Taken,' by Robert Frost."

"Two roads diverged in a yellow wood,
And sorry I could not travel both . . ."

While the chaplain recites the poem, Doomsday begins to sob quietly. I lower my head, remembering the tattoo on Will's arm, and how that poem brought us together. I think about Will's life, too, and how he really did take the road less traveled.

But do I? No. I'd be a hypocrite if I said I did. If only I could go back, change the way I acted the last time I saw Will. At least he would have known that I cared. But what good does wishful thinking do now?

When the chaplain finishes, he puts away the sheet of paper and opens his Bible.

"Today, I'd also like to celebrate Will's life by reading a passage from God's Word. The Gospel of John, chapter eight, verses three through seven."

I look up, wondering if I heard right.

"'The teachers of the law and the pharisees brought in a woman caught in adultery. . . .'"

I feel a tingling on the back of my neck. I glance around. Quindlan and Hawk have their heads bowed, but Doomsday is looking straight at me. I feel dizzy, light-headed. I plant my feet and stare at the ground until the chaplain finishes. "'If any of you is without sin, let him be the first to throw a stone.'"

The chaplain bends down, picks up a handful of dirt, and sprinkles it over Will's casket. "'Remember, O man, that you are dust, and to dust you shall return.' Please, everyone, join me."

Doomsday is the first to stoop down and pick up a handful of dirt. He sprinkles it over the casket. The rest of us do the same. The sound is like heavy rain falling against a rooftop. "'I am the resurrection and the life,'" the chaplain drones on. "'He who believes in me will live, though he dies.'" He closes with the Twenty-third Psalm. "'The Lord is my shepherd; I shall not want . . .'"

"Noah?" Hawk whispers. "Hey, I'm not going to hang around and watch Will get buried. It's too depressing. Do you need a ride home?"

"Oh, no thanks. I'm going to stay a little longer. But, Hawk?" I glance at Quindlan, who's speaking with the chaplain, and Doomsday, who's kneeling beside Will's grave. "Do you know who gave the chaplain that Bible passage to read? The one about the woman caught in adultery?"

"No, I don't. It was strange, wasn't it? Sure didn't make sense for a burial. Anyway, don't hang around this place too long. I'll see you at school. Take it easy, man."

Doomsday leans precariously over the hole in the ground. His lips are moving like he's whispering something to Will. I walk over, listen closely, and make out bits and pieces from Walt Whitman's *Leaves of Grass*.

> *"Every year shall you bloom again,*
> *Out from where you retired*
> *you shall emerge again . . ."*

When he's finished, he stands and marches down the hill. I watch until he disappears.

"Noah?" I turn around. It's Quindlan. From the corner of my eye, I see the chaplain heading toward the funeral home.

"Hey," I say. "Where's Doomsday going?"

"Oh, he's got some unfinished business here. But tell me, how've you been?"

"Um, not too good."

"Yeah. It's been a rough week. Every afternoon I find myself looking for Will. I keep thinking he's going to turn the corner on the Drag, wave to me, hang out for a while. Doomsday's been a wreck too. I still can't believe Will's gone."

"Me neither." I look around and lower my voice. "So, how's the investigation going? Did they find anything new from the autopsy?"

Quindlan sighs. "No, not really. The medical examiner said Will was strangled, like Kyle and Paul, but that was obvious from the start. One strange thing, though, is that the cross on his chest was carved about three or four hours after he died, which is different from the other two murders. Kyle's and Paul's carvings were done immediately. So the killer either stayed with Will for a while, or left and then went back to the crime scene. In all three cases, though, the guy was very professional. Highly experienced. What they call an organized killer. He left no DNA behind, no fingerprints. Nothing."

"So, in other words, they still don't know much?" I say.

"Right. But I do have a little inside information."

"Really? What?"

"Well, I spoke with the FBI profiler yesterday. Turns out,

there's some evidence he doesn't want released to the public just yet. Right now they have reason to believe Warren Banks killed both Kyle and Paul. Paul was murdered twenty-four hours before the police arrested Banks, and that's why Banks is still in custody. But it's possible that someone else—maybe another member of the Westboro group—killed Will. Anyway, they've got some leads now. It's just a matter of time."

"Another member from Westboro? So they think there may be a group behind the murders?"

"It's possible. A group that believes they're doing God's will by exterminating evil. Specifically, gay teenagers." He shakes his head. "Maybe they figured no one would care if they preyed on gay foster kids."

"God, that's so sick. Anyway, I hope you're right. I hope the detectives know what they're doing."

In the distance I hear a dog barking. I peer across the cemetery and see Hercules chained to a tree.

"I better go," Quindlan says. "Just call me if you need to talk. And visit me anytime. You know where I hang out."

"Quindlan? Wait. I need to ask you something. Do you know why the chaplain read from John, chapter eight?"

"That was Doomsday's idea. He used to read to us from the Bible from time to time, and that story caught Will's attention. He liked it a lot. Said he could relate to the woman caught in adultery—how she was nameless, alone, and how the religious leaders wanted to stone her. And he liked the way Jesus answered them: 'He who is without sin, let him cast the first stone.'"

"Yeah," I say. "I like that too."

"And there was something else," Quindlan says. "Will wondered what Jesus wrote in the sand. He said it must have been something beautiful, like a poem. For some reason, that always stuck with me. With Doomsday, too. Anyway, why do you ask?"

I think about Will's book hidden under my bed. The book I can't tell a soul about—especially Quindlan. Not that he wouldn't understand—I think he would—but the fact is he's a cop. One who's serious about his job. If push came to shove, he could arrest me. "Well, it just didn't make sense," I say. "It's not a passage you usually hear at a burial."

"You're right. In fact, I think we upset the chaplain a little." He smiles. "But, hey, I'm glad you came today, Noah. Guess Hawk invited you."

"Yeah. He seems like a decent guy."

Quindlan shakes his head. "Don't be so sure. Remember what I said. If you see him around school, stay far away. He's not a person you want to associate with."

As Quindlan takes off, I hear voices. Soon three men appear. Gravediggers. They begin shoveling dirt onto Will's casket, talking about what they're going to have for lunch, laughing as they work. Hawk was right. This is too depressing.

The wind kicks up. I zipper my jacket and pull up the hood. I'm alone now, with time to kill and a lot of thinking to do. I walk along the path and read some of the nearby headstones.

BABY GIRL
NOV 2, 2006

I stop, realizing that the date must be a record of her birth *and* death. A stillborn. The plain headstone is covered with dead leaves and grass. I wonder if anyone visits her. I move along.

JIMMY
2007

No last name. No year of his birth, only his death. Probably a homeless guy, like Doomsday. I wonder if he had a tragic story too.

Strangely, the next stone contains a long list of names but only one date.

"Hey!" I call to the gravediggers. "Can I ask you guys something?"

One of them sighs, sets down his shovel, and walks over to me.

"What does this mean?" I ask. "Why so many names, but just one date?"

He studies the headstone for a moment. "That's what we call a mass burial."

Mass burial? I picture scenes from Auschwitz—a heap of dead bodies lying on top of each other. "You mean . . . they all died on the same day?"

"No. If no one claims a body, it's cremated. The ashes get stored over there." He points to what looks like a shed in the distance. "When there's no room left, we bury their ashes together. It saves time and space."

"Oh. Okay. Well, thanks."

He goes back to work. I walk a few more paces, and

when I see the next two headstones, side by side, I stop dead in my tracks.

KYLE LESTER **PAUL MATEO**
1992–2010   **1994–2010**

I stand there for a long time, trying to make sense of this. Suddenly everything is quiet. The wind has died down, the gravediggers have left, and I hear footsteps behind me. I turn around and see Doomsday. "Hello, Noah. I saw you walking around. I wanted to make sure you were all right."

"Oh, yeah. I'm okay."

He takes my hand. "Can I introduce you to someone? She's waiting just down the hill."

"Um, sure."

He gives me a quick smile and motions for me to follow him. As we walk down the hill, I notice again how the landscape changes. The graves in this section are well kept, and there are clusters of cut fresh flowers, as well as planted mums and daisies.

Doomsday stops and points to a grave. "Here she is. My fiancée. Mary Turner."

"Oh." I stop and read the stone.

MARY TURNER
1948–1966
BELOVED WIFE
I LOVE YOU, I LOVE YOU, IS MY SONG
AND HERE MY SILLINESS BEGINS.
—PABLO NERUDA

"I took liberty and called her my wife," Doomsday says. "But we weren't married yet. The quote is from the first poem she ever read to me. 'Love Song,' by Pablo Neruda. Of course, she recited it in Spanish at the time. It hadn't been translated yet."

"I know the poem," I say. "It's beautiful."

"Yes, it is."

The two of us are quiet for a while. Finally I say, "Quindlan told me what happened to Mary."

"Yes. Charles Whitman, the UT sniper, killed her. Mary and I were students at the time. So in love. She was studying Spanish literature and was going to be a poet. She was shot right on Guadalupe Street. I was there. She died in my arms."

"I'm so sorry."

He nods. "Mary was five months pregnant. Her family was very religious and when they found out, they disowned her, even though we were engaged. Things were quite different back then. But still, I blame myself."

"Why would you blame yourself?" I say. "There was nothing you could have done."

He sighs. "Maybe so. But God works in mysterious ways, Noah. I'm sure your father's taught you that. God took her in order to punish me."

"What? No, that's not true. I don't believe God punishes people. God is *love*. That's what it says in the Bible. You know that."

He looks at me, shakes his head sadly, then kneels down and runs a hand over the stone.

I kneel beside him. "Doomsday? Sometimes bad things just happen. Like you losing Mary and the baby. And like

Will getting killed. Will was a kind and good person. He didn't do anything to deserve that."

Doomsday doesn't answer for a long time. Finally he says, "Like I said, Noah, God works in mysterious ways."

"What do you mean?"

"Will was a talented boy, a lovely soul, and a good friend. But only God can see into a man's heart. I'm not the one to pass judgment."

I study Doomsday for a while. He seems lost in his own sadness. "Doomsday? Is that why you preach on the Drag? Because you think you did something wrong? Something to cause Mary's death?"

He nods. "Yes, I suppose that's why. It's a form of penance."

"Penance? What about forgiveness?"

He doesn't answer.

"Doomsday?"

He looks up. His eyes are red and filled with tears. "I don't know anything about forgiveness, Noah." He dries his eyes with his sleeve and continues brushing his fingers over the stone. "You should run along now. I'm going to visit with Mary awhile longer."

I don't know what to say, so I place a hand on Doomsday's shoulder. "Don't stay out here too long, man. It's getting cold." I stand up. The barren landscape around Will's grave appears even bleaker than it did earlier.

"Doomsday, can I ask you something?"

"Yes."

"Why are certain people buried in that barren area, up the hill? Like the two other foster boys who were murdered, and a baby with no name, and a guy who's just called Jimmy?"

Doomsday peers into the distance. "That part of the cemetery is owned by the city. It's for people whose bodies haven't been claimed. If I didn't have a plot right here next to Mary, that's probably where I'd wind up." He sighs. "Some people call it Potter's Field."

A cold wind blows. Sweat prickles under my arms. "Potter's Field?"

"Yes. It's a term from the Bible. I'm sure you know the story. After Judas betrayed Jesus for thirty pieces of silver, Judas realized the mistake he'd made, threw the coins onto the temple floor, then went out and hanged himself. Because the silver was blood money, the priests weren't allowed to put it into the temple treasury, so they used it to buy the potter's field. A place where they buried foreigners."

"Also called field of blood," I say.

"Yes, that's right." He shakes his head. "Like Judas, we all have blood on our hands."

{seventeen}

"THERE'S A name for this, you know," Carson says.

"Really?" I'm sitting on the floor in the DPCP's weight room, flipping through Will's book while Carson makes a sorry attempt at a military press. "What is it?"

He grunts loudly and heaves the barbell back onto the rack. "Schizophrenia."

In the corner of the room is a pile of prosthetic limbs, left over from the DPCP's last business trip. I'm tempted to grab one of the rubberized legs—the kind that bend at the knee—and wring Carson's neck. "Come on, Carson! Look, I showed you the weird poem, the John eight Bible passage, the cemetery *phone number*. You got to admit, something's up. This is *not* normal."

Carson shakes his head and sits up. Unfortunately for me, he's not wearing a T-shirt, and his not-so-toned abs bulge over his sweatpants. "Listen, Noah, first you tell me that Quindlan's an undercover cop, which is hard enough to believe, and now—"

"Dude, I am *not* making this up! Quindlan was at the crime scene. All the investigators knew him. Plus, we talked. God, I knew I shouldn't have told you! I swear, Carson, if you say a word to anyone, or if you let Quindlan know that I told you—"

"My lips are sealed. No worries, Noah, you can trust me. And fine, whatever, maybe Quindlan really is an undercover cop, but now you're telling me that some psycho wrote a poem in Will's book, *after* he killed him, while he was waiting to carve a cross on his chest? I mean, really, dude, what am I supposed to think except that you're going nuts?"

"Fine. Don't believe me. I don't care."

"All right, all right, maybe I'm not being fair. Look, I know you've been through a lot, Noah, but will you forget about that book for a minute and listen to me?"

Suddenly I feel really tired. Like I've been running for hours and I'm about to collapse. I set down the book and fix my eyes on Carson. "Yeah, sure."

"Okay, here's how I see it. Nothing makes sense, right? We got to know Will, and he was cool. We liked him. He was our friend. Next thing we know, he's dead. Murdered by some homophobic crazy guy. Worst of all, you're the one who found his body, and that totally sucks. Plus you're feeling guilty because you gave him the brush-off. So now you're trying to find answers in a book? I think you need to leave it alone, Noah. Move on."

"But you don't get it, Carson. You weren't there when I found Will. You didn't talk to the police. You didn't see what I saw. And today, at the burial, the whole thing was freaky. I don't see how any of it could be just a co-incidence."

Carson leans over, picks up Will's book, and turns to the page I've dog-eared—the one with the Lead Belly song and the Potter's Field poem. "All right, what if Will wrote this poem right around the time of Kyle Lester's burial? Or even Paul Mateo's? Wouldn't that explain the cemetery phone number, the references to the homeless, stillborn, Potter's Field, and all that?"

I shrug. "Yeah, maybe."

"Plus, you said John eight was Will's favorite Bible passage. At least, that's what Quindlan told you, right? Maybe Will jotted it on that page for a reason. A reason only he knew."

"I've thought of all that. But how do you explain the different handwriting? And why is it written on the page with the Lead Belly song? That was the day I met Will. I *sang* it for him. I saw him write the lyrics in the book."

Carson studies me. "Noah, you're seriously scaring me now. Because if you believe some psycho killer wrote this poem, and that he wrote it on *this* particular page for a reason—because it was the day you met Will—then you would have to believe he wrote it specifically *for you*."

"Yeah, I know."

"And you think that's possible?"

I hesitate for a moment. "It could be."

Carson throws up his hands. "Oh, man. I don't know

what to say. What if . . . what if you brought the book to school and showed it to Hawk? Maybe he'd be able to explain it. Maybe it would all make sense."

"Hawk? I don't know. I don't know if I can trust him. Honestly, I'm not sure I can trust anyone." Carson is looking at me like I'm completely insane.

I shake my head. "Don't worry about me, all right? I'm *not* going crazy. I swear. I know this whole thing is nuts, but right now I just need to find out the truth. Maybe it's nothing, but maybe it's not. I just . . . I have to know, that's all."

Carson frowns and tosses the book onto my lap. "Do yourself a favor, Noah. *Burn* this thing. Or give it to the police, which was what you should have done in the first place."

"Thanks for the great advice. You *know* I can't give it to the police. First they'd charge me for tampering with evidence, and then they'd probably send me to a psychiatrist." I sigh and shove the book into my back pocket. Carson is right about one thing. I need to give it a rest. At least for now.

"Fine. Suit yourself." Carson picks up a set of dumbbells and begins doing curls. A few seconds later, there's a knock on the door. "Carson? Are you in there?" It's the DPCP. Oh, joy.

"Yeah, Dad, come in. Noah's here too."

Slowly, Carson's father enters the room. He looks flustered. "Oh, Noah, hello. Carson told me what happened to your friend. And I've seen the story on the news. I'm very sorry."

"Yeah," I say. "Thanks."

I've never seen the DPCP so uncomfortable before. I guess he's feeling pretty guilty for how he treated Will. I hope there will be some poetic justice to suit his crime, like Prosthetics Inc. plummeting on Wall Street, or maybe a company tax audit. Yeah, that would work.

"Um, Carson?" he says. "The manager from Guitar Center just phoned. He asked if you would pick up a shift tomorrow. Apparently someone called in sick. I told him you'd get back to him."

"Oh, all right." Carson sets down the dumbbells. "Let's see. . . . I'm going to church in the morning, but I can work after that. Thanks, Dad. I'll let him know."

The DPCP winces at the church comment, then manages a small smile. "Great. Well, I'm glad to see someone's putting this weight room to use. I'll, uh, have the housekeeper clean up those limbs in the corner."

"That's all right, Dad. I'll do it. In fact, I'll put them in the trunk and take them back to the factory for you."

"Thank you, Carson. That's very thoughtful."

As the DPCP exits the room, Carson arches an eyebrow at me. "Pretty amazing, huh? He's, like, almost human."

"Yeah, how'd that happen?"

He shrugs. "It's this job I got."

"Oh, right, I meant to ask you, how'd it go today?"

"Really good. The manager is cool. He likes me a lot. The best part is, they've got these *sweet* vintage guitars all over the store, and I get to play them when it's slow. I'm working those angles I talked about too. We'll have another gig set up pretty soon. You know, when you're ready. And get this: when I came home today, I told the DPCP how I networked with the clientele, and now he's calling me an entrepreneur."

"Wow. Unbelievable."

"Yeah, and he's starting to lay off about me going to church. Only, I haven't told him about the baptism yet. That could get a little hairy."

"So you're really going through with it?"

"Yeah. In a few weeks I'll be getting dunked in Kat's backyard pool. I was going to wait until summer, but I figured, the pool's heated and she's even got a Jacuzzi, so I won't freeze my ass off. Plus, I'm ready. I really want to do it. And, Noah, the youth group's having a party afterward. I hope you'll come."

I picture Aubrey and Brandon, side by side in the bubbly Jacuzzi, sipping virgin strawberry daiquiris and singing glory hallelujahs for Carson's new leap of faith. "Gee, sounds like a great time," I say. But Carson's so high on Jesus he doesn't even catch my sarcasm.

"Yep. And while we're on the subject, I was hoping you'd do me a favor."

I hold up both hands. "Hey, I already did the dunk. When I was seven. And stupid. And severely brainwashed. I'm not doing it again."

"No, that's not what I meant." He picks up the dumbbells and starts a new set of curls. "I need a workout buddy. I've only got a few weeks to get in shape. I want to look buff for Kat, you know, when I rise up out of the water. So what do you say?"

I stare at him in disbelief. "Please tell me you're joking."

"No. I'm serious. I was even thinking of untangling my

dreads for the occasion. It would be majorly painful, but I want my hair to look good when it's wet."

I've had about all I can take. "Are you planning to wear your Speedo, too?"

He stops curling. His eyes open wide. "Should I?"

It takes every ounce of my self-control for me to keep from throttling him. "All right, explain something to me. Are you getting baptized because you got born again, or are you hoping Kat won't be able to resist your bod in a swimsuit?"

He sets down the weights. "All right, I guess I was getting carried away. But, Noah, I'm serious about this. Getting baptized means a lot to me. Like I told you before, I really have found God, and Jesus, and, well, it's like I don't even hate my father anymore. That's *huge*. And what's weird is that *he* hasn't changed; it's *me*. I've changed. And the people at youth group, they pray for me. No one's ever done that before. It's pretty cool."

"Okay, okay. I get it. I'm glad you found God, Carson. Really. The thing you need to understand about me is that I never lost him."

Carson smiles. "Yeah, I see what you mean. Anyway, how about we start our workout tomorrow? You can show me the baseball players' routine in the weight room. And, as an added bonus, it'll get your mind off that book."

† † †

On the way home, I begin to think that maybe I *am* going crazy. Maybe I've imagined this whole thing. Maybe I

148

should burn the book. That would be the best way to get rid of it. But no, I couldn't destroy Will's poems. It wouldn't be right. They're all that's left of him.

My mom's in the kitchen cooking dinner when I return. My dad's in the den, poring over some doorstop Bible commentary. Quietly, I pad up the stairs before either of them sees me. I pass Melanie's room and hear her playing with a friend. I close my door, and before stashing Will's book beneath my bed, I decide to check out one more thing. September ninth. The day Kyle Lester was murdered. Just a sanity check, I tell myself. I sit down and find the page.

There it is. A poem.

For Kyle
Religion and hate—
longtime friends
who share the same fate.
What we can be, they dictate.
Who we can love, they mandate.
Why can't we just be,
and wipe the slate
clean?

In the margin, written in lighter, shaky ink:

One Small Act of Kindness
*Who would have thought
my first victim
would be a penniless boy
offering up a meal?*

Who would have thought
one small act of kindness
would lead to his
death?
Easy,
way too easy.
And now
I want more.

My head reels. It all goes together. The poem Will wrote about Kyle. The poem the killer wrote about Kyle. I shut the book and quickly shove it under my bed. It feels like I've touched something evil, something so dark it scares me. Could there really be someone messing with my head? As I sit there with my heart pounding, I hear my mother call, "John? Please come here. You need to see this."

I run downstairs. My parents are in the family room. "Noah? When did you get home?" my mom asks.

"Just a little while ago." I look at the TV. News 8 Austin is on, and Warren Banks's mug shot is back up on the screen.

"A suicide watch has been placed on Warren Banks, suspect in the murder of Austin teenager Kyle Lester. Earlier today, Banks tried to hang himself in the shower with an electrical cord at the Travis County Jail. The police are still awaiting DNA results in the murder case, and if Banks is tried and convicted, he could face the death penalty."

While the newscaster shows clips from the Westboro Baptist Church's God Hates Fags march, I begin to realize what I need to do. "Dad?"

"Yes?" He looks startled. I've barely spoken to my father since the night Will had dinner with us, but now I need his help.

"I want to talk to Warren Banks. Face to face. I need to know if he was the caller, and if he's the one who killed Kyle and Paul. It's important. Please."

"Noah," my mom says, "you've been through enough. John? Please tell Noah that's not an option."

My father looks at me. He doesn't say anything for a while. Finally he nods. "All right. Wait here. It's best for me to look the part, so I'll dig out my minister's collar. We'll go tonight."

{eighteen}

"LET ME talk to the guards," my dad says. "And remember, whatever I say, just play along."

I've never been inside a prison before. The first thing I notice is the smell. Kind of like the inside of a Roach Motel. Bright lights bounce off the walls, causing my eyes to throb. Everything is stale, rectangular, generic. Ahead I see visitors lined up in cubicles, speaking into clunky black phones sprouting heavy metal cords. A thick sheet of Plexiglas separates us from the inmates. No touching allowed.

"Yes, that's right," my father says to one of the guards. "Warren Banks. We need to visit with him in a private room. Yes, I know he's on suicide watch, and that's why we're here. He needs help. As you can see, I'm a minister."

Besides being a Christian radio guru, my dad went to seminary and got one of those divinity degrees. So even though he's not a pastor of a church, he's still qualified to perform weddings and funerals and get up close and personal with the criminally insane.

"All right," the guard says. "But the boy has to wait here." He looks me up and down, like I'm one of the roaches in his sleazy prison motel.

"No," my father says. "My son comes with me."

"I'm sorry, sir, but that's not possi—"

"John Nordstrom? Is that you?" A man in uniform steps out of the main office. His badge reads LIEUTENANT JEFFREY JONES. I'm guessing he's got more clout than the guard who's big on enforcing the rules. He shakes hands with my dad and smiles. "What do you know? The Bible Answer Guy in the flesh. What brings you here this evening?"

This is the kind of stuff that happens all the time when I go places with my father. He's a real celebrity in the Bible Belt.

The guard's mouth falls open. "I'm . . . sorry, sir. I had no idea."

"Oh, no problem at all," my dad says. "It's good to see you, Jeffrey. This is my son, Noah. The two of us were about to visit one of your inmates, Warren Banks. You may have heard he'd been a member of our church a while back. We just found out about his suicide attempt. The whole thing is so unfortunate. Anyway"—he reaches over and pats me on the back—"Noah is seriously considering going into the ministry, and I thought talking with Banks would be a good experience for him."

I'm so shocked I can't speak. My father, proud upholder of the Ten Commandments, has just told a lie. A big one.

Lieutenant Jones is rather impressed. "Is that so? Following in your father's footsteps, hey? Well, good for you, Noah. Henry, please show them in," he says to the guard. "And don't worry, we've got tight security in the visiting rooms—two-way mirrors, audio recorders, armed guards in the hallways. No reason for concern."

Oh yeah? And what if you've got the wrong guy locked up? What if the real killer is still out on the streets?

My dad and I follow Henry past the row of cubicles. There's a girl about Melanie's age visiting one of the inmates. She's sitting on a woman's lap and has a phone pressed to her ear. She's singing "Billy Boy" into the receiver. The man behind the Plexiglas watches the girl and smiles sadly. He lifts one hand and touches five fingers to the glass; the girl reaches up and matches him, finger for finger.

Henry's huge wad of keys jingles loudly with each step he takes. He opens a door, leads us through, and locks it behind us. As we walk down the long, narrow hallway, I whisper to my father, "The ministry? Are you kidding me?"

He shrugs. "Your life is a ministry, Noah. Don't you know that?"

We pass through several more doors, and each time, Henry leads us through one and locks it behind us. I feel like a rat in a maze. Finally he tells us to wait outside a room. He's going to get Warren Banks.

After about ten minutes I'm feeling really claustrophobic. My palms are sweaty, I can barely breathe, and I have an intense desire to make a run for it. Suddenly the door opens. Inside the room, Warren Banks is sitting on a metal chair, looking down at the floor. He's wearing an orange jumpsuit, and there are several bandages taped to his neck. We walk in and take seats across from him. For some reason I'm expecting Banks to be handcuffed, but he's not, which scares me a little. I try not to think about Hannibal Lecter—his mask, his sharp teeth.

Henry says, "I'll be right outside, Mr. Nordstrom." He exits the room but, thank goodness, leaves the door wide open.

"Hello, Warren," my dad says.

Banks doesn't answer. He doesn't even look up.

"I hope you're well."

Hope you're well? Come on, Dad. We live in Texas—the number one state for executions. It's like asking a guy sitting in the electric chair if he's comfortable with high voltage.

My father clears his throat and continues. "I believe you've met my son, Noah, at King of Glory Christian Center. My daughter, Melanie, was in your Sunday school class. We heard you were in trouble, and thought you might like some company."

Something like a snort escapes Banks's throat. After that, a very long minute goes by. Slowly, he lifts his head. I can tell you right now, if you try to hang yourself and don't succeed, it does a number on you. His face is dotted with a million purple bruises, and his eyes are swollen, veined, and red. I hate to think what's under his bandages. "Company? Please, Mr. Nordstrom. Don't patronize me." He fixes his eyes on me. "Besides, I *know* why you're here."

My heart pounds. "You do?"

"Yeah. So, please, just get on with it. Say your piece and leave."

I look at my father. He shrugs and motions for me to continue. Only, I have no clue what to say. "We heard about your . . . your accident, and—"

"You mean my suicide attempt. Call it what it is, all right?"

"Okay. We heard about your suicide attempt. And I was wondering . . . why, you know . . ."

"Why I did it?"

"Yes."

He shakes his head. "Jeez, you guys are all the same. Un-believable." He looks at me defiantly. "Why do you *think* I did it?"

The question hangs in midair. The room is deathly quiet. I can hear my father's nose whistling.

"I don't know. Because you killed someone? Because you killed Kyle Lester? And maybe the other foster kid, Paul Mateo?"

His eyebrows shoot up. He starts to laugh. Only, it's the kind of laugh that's not amused at all. "Is that what you believe?"

"Listen, Warren," my father interrupts. He sounds pretty pissed. "We didn't come here for this. Noah's been through a pretty rough ordeal. He's the one who found the body of the third foster boy—Will Reed—the one killed in the woods along the greenbelt. And he had some questions, that's all. If you don't want to talk with us, we'll leave right now."

Banks blinks a few times. He looks stunned. "No . . . please, don't go. Stay." His voice is different now. Softer.

Almost desperate. "Noah? I'm sorry. I had no idea it was you who found the body. Is that really why you came here? To talk about the murders?"

"Yeah."

"And no other reason?"

"No."

"All right, then. Go ahead. Ask whatever you want."

"Okay." I take a deep breath and try to gather my thoughts. I have no idea where to begin. "Well, about a week before Kyle Lester was killed, there was this caller on my father's show. Maybe you heard him. He spewed a lot of antigay stuff."

"Yes. I remember the guy. How could I forget?" He pauses for a moment; then a look of understanding spreads across his face. "Oh, so you thought the caller was me?"

"I thought . . . well, yeah."

He shrugs. "It's all right. I don't blame you. It makes sense. I mean, I'm sure you've heard about my involvement with the Westboro Baptist Church. It's been all over the news, and it's not something I'm proud of. Anyway, now that I think about it, when I found out Kyle was dead, and I heard about the cross carved on his chest and the note left with his body, I immediately thought of that caller. I thought he might have had something to do with it."

"Yeah, me too," I say.

"Actually, we both did," my father says.

"The sad thing is," Banks goes on, "I used to believe a lot of the stuff that caller said. It kills me to think of it now. How brainwashed I was. But the answer's no. It wasn't me. And for whatever it's worth, I didn't kill Kyle. Or the other boy, Paul. The police keep questioning me about him, trying to pin another murder on me. I didn't even know Paul."

I don't know if Banks's statement is true, but for now I decide to go along with it. "That's what Marty said. I saw him a few weeks ago. He told me he came to visit you. He said you were with Kyle the night he was killed, but that Kyle left with someone else. A man asking for spare change."

"Yes, that's right. Pastor Simpson came too, and I told him the same thing. I think both he and Marty believed me. At least, I hope they did. I know Pastor Simpson has been going through a hard time because of me. Because I used to be a member of King of Glory. Apparently the police and the media have been hounding him with questions."

"I heard. But, Warren, the man who left with Kyle—I was wondering if you might be able to tell me what he looked like."

Banks shakes his head. "It was dark. And I didn't pay much attention. But . . . hold on, why do you want to know this?" He looks at my dad. A glimmer of hope lights up his face. "Is there another suspect? Do they have someone else in custody?"

"I'm sorry, Warren," my father says. "No. At least, not that I'm aware of."

Banks closes his eyes for a moment. "Oh, wishful thinking on my part."

The guard appears at the door. "Five more minutes."

"Noah," Banks says, "the boy you found at the greenbelt—Will Reed—was he a friend of yours?"

"Yes, he was."

"I'm very sorry."

"Yeah. Me too."

My dad puts a hand on my shoulder. My first impulse is to shrug it off, but I don't. No one says anything for a while. "It's hard to lose a friend," Banks says. "Kyle and I weren't close or anything, but he was a nice guy. And for whatever it's worth, we weren't, you know, intimate. I just liked him as a friend. That's all. I think he liked me too. We talked a lot. I mean, sure, he got into some trouble, which isn't surprising, seeing he didn't have a family, but deep down he was just scared and alone. Like me."

Banks shifts his feet, and that's when I notice the chain. His ankles are shackled together.

"Noah?" I look up. "I'm very sorry about your friend. And I apologize, too, Mr. Nordstrom, for being so rude when you first came. You see, I thought you were with the Exodus group."

"Exodus group?" I say. "What's that?"

Banks doesn't answer. He looks at my dad.

"Exodus is a national evangelical organization," my father explains. "King of Glory has a chapter. Their goal is to help people who want to change their sexual orientation. The name Exodus is derived from when Moses led the people of Israel out of slavery and into the Promised Land."

"Change their sexual orientation?" I say. "That's insane."

"Yes, I agree," Banks says. "Anyway, it seems I'm their new project. Just the other day, a guy from King of Glory came to visit. He told me he used to be gay. But now he's given his life over to God, and he's happily married to a woman, and they have two beautiful children." There's bitterness in his voice. He sighs deeply. "I'm not proud of this either, but after he left, well, that's when I . . ." He trails off.

"That's when you tried to kill yourself," my father says.

"Yeah. Only, it didn't work. Obviously. I'm still here."

From the corner of my eye, I see my father swallow hard.

"After Kyle was murdered and I was arrested," Banks says, "I believed what that caller on your show said—that God had brought judgment on both of us. Pretty crazy, huh? I mean, all Kyle wanted to do was help someone in need. Buy him a meal. Anyway, I've been thinking about this for a long time, and maybe you can answer a question for me, Mr. Nordstrom."

"I don't know, Warren," my dad says. "I can try."

"Okay. You see, I love God. I always have. I've only had one relationship with a man, and I really loved him, but I ended it, because I believed it was a sin. Now he's with someone else. I've given my life to God, over and over, begged him to change me, but I'm still the same. I'm still gay. Can you explain that, Mr. Nordstrom?"

My father doesn't say anything for a long time. Finally he looks up. His eyes are glassy. "I wish I had an answer, Warren, but I don't. There was a time, not too long ago, when I thought I knew everything, but it seems I know very little. I'd say it's between you and God now. But please, don't try to hurt yourself again. That's certainly not the answer."

A few seconds later, the guard walks into the room. "Visiting time is over," he barks. "I need to escort Mr. Banks back to his cell."

Slowly, Banks stands. He shakes my dad's hand first,

then mine. "Thanks for coming." He follows the guard to the door, but before leaving the room, he turns around. "There's something I forgot to mention, Noah. It's about the man who left with Kyle. I didn't get a good look at his face, but I can tell you one thing. He was carrying a Bible."

{nineteen}

"LOOK, I know you're pissed off at me, and you have every right to be. It's just . . . I *really* need to talk to you."

I'm at church, sitting directly behind Aubrey, whispering into her ear. Her father, Pastor Simpson, has just finished his sermon; I watch as he briskly walks up the aisle past us. Now the worship team take their places onstage and are about to sing their last sappy inspirational song. "Everyone, please rise!" commands the leader. "Let's praise the Lord together!"

Carson is next to me, right behind Kat. Immediately, he bolts up from his chair and joins in, belting out the chorus, "Jesus, you're all I need!"

"Aubrey, please don't ignore me," I say. Her hair brushes against my cheek. God, she smells good. I glance down and remember kissing the curve of her collarbone that fatal afternoon in the woods at the youth retreat. "I'm sorry about the night at the Red Room. The song—it was a mistake."

Slowly, she turns around. Her face is flushed. I'm hoping it's because she feels the same chemistry as I do, but I doubt it. "A mistake?"

"Yeah, a big one."

The congregation sings, *"You shed your blood for me . . ."*

"Explain," she says.

"Paid the price so I can be . . ."

"Here? Now?"

"In your fold eternally . . ."

"Yes."

While the rest of the church sings the chorus, I say, "Okay. The song I wrote was the exact opposite of how I feel. I thought you might see through it, you know, to the cryptic message. It was . . . well, it was my friend Will who gave me the idea."

The song ends. As people are saying their last Amens, Aubrey looks at me. I can tell she's holding back tears. "I'm sorry, Noah," she whispers. "Carson told me what happened. It must have been awful. I just . . . well, I was angry before, but I should have called you. Are you okay?"

"Actually, I'm not."

She glances around the church. "Come on, let's get out of here."

"Now?"

"Yeah." As the congregation begins its "meet and greet" session, she brushes past Brandon and motions for me to follow. I do. Brandon doesn't look too happy about this turn of events, and I can't say that I care.

When we reach the aisle, Aubrey grabs my hand. Everyone is staring at us now. My guess is that about half the congregation knows it was me who found the body of the third gay foster boy. The media didn't release my name, but word travels fast in King of Glory. From the corner of my eye, I see Pastor Simpson. I can tell he's not meditating on Jesus's shed blood right now; I think he might enjoy shedding some of mine instead. We race past him and out the door.

† † †

Aubrey and I stand together in the woods at the greenbelt, gazing at what's left of Will's campsite—the charred fire pit, a small knot of rope left from the makeshift clothesline, the stub of Hawk's cigarette, the big rock where Will and I sat and composed my anti-love song. Meanwhile I fill Aubrey in on the past three crazy weeks of my life. She listens intently, barely saying a word.

When I finish, we're both quiet for a long time. I hear the familiar sounds of water rushing over the rocks, cicadas chirring. It's oddly peaceful. Aubrey was the one who decided we should come here. She wanted to understand exactly what I saw the morning I found Will.

Finally she says, "Noah? Where was the body?"

"I'll show you." I take Aubrey's hand and lead her to the spot. It's covered with leaves and twigs, like nothing ever happened. "Right here. Will was facedown. For a second I wasn't sure he was dead, but then I knew."

"And the note with the Bible verse? Where was that?"

"Right there. Beside Will's head. Tucked under a big rock. The rope was next to it."

"And what about . . . ?"

"The carving? I saw that too. Will was wearing a T-shirt I'd given him. You know the one. The Kinks' 1985 tour. The front was stained with blood. I lifted it, and the cross was there. You can tell the killer took his time. It was no rush job."

"Oh, God. You must have been so scared, Noah."

"I think I felt more shock than anything. It took some time to sink in."

Aubrey shudders. "I just don't understand how anyone could be so sick. I saw those people on TV—from the Westboro group. I had no idea they existed. And they call themselves a *church*. The whole thing's insane. And to think that Warren Banks left King of Glory and joined them. I just don't get it."

"Me neither. Especially after talking to him in jail. He seemed pretty tortured, but it's hard to imagine him killing anyone. Anyway, the police don't know for sure if the Westboro church is involved, or if Warren Banks is guilty of the first two murders. At this point the killer could be anywhere."

Aubrey thinks this over. "You're right. I mean, it's possible that one man killed all three boys—Kyle, Paul, *and* Will—and that the police have no idea who it is."

"It's possible."

It's a relief to finally talk things over, and I'm glad Aubrey's with me, but still the guilt hangs over me. Especially here, the place where I blew Will off, the place where he died. I run my hand across his book, tucked away in my front pocket. "Hey, Aubrey? Did you know that our church had one of those Exodus groups? I mean, before I told you all this stuff."

She sighs. "Yeah. I knew."

"And what do you think of it?"

"I hate it. I think it sucks." She looks at me. "The truth is, Noah, I used to believe everything my father taught. But I don't anymore. I never told you this, but I met this guy Danny in theater arts. He was my mime partner, and we got to be pretty good friends. When he found out my father was a pastor, he told me that he used to belong to the youth group at his church. Only, when he came out this year, told the group he was gay, they were horrified. They decided to have a prayer meeting for him, and when he didn't show up, they told him not to come around unless he was willing to change. It's just so *wrong*. I don't think Marty would *ever* do something like that."

"You're right. He wouldn't. Carson told me Marty doesn't agree with the church's view that being gay is a sin. He thinks the youth group might be able to bring about some kind of change."

"Really? That's great."

A lock of hair has fallen into Aubrey's face. I reach over and tuck it behind her ear. "Aubrey, there's something I didn't tell you. Something about me and Will. You see, when we first met, I didn't know he was gay. But after we hung out for a while, I realized he was, well, *into* me. Actually it was Carson who figured it out. Anyway, I thought I was okay with it. Will knew I was straight, and it's not like he was expecting anything in return. But it turns out, I wasn't okay. The last time I saw him, right here in the woods, he said something and I took it the wrong way. I'm really ashamed of how I acted toward him. I was going to apologize at the Red Room, but he never showed up."

Aubrey takes my hand. "I'm sorry, Noah. Try not to dwell on it. I'm sure Will knew how you really felt."

"That's the problem. I'll never know." I bend down, pick up a rock, throw it as hard as I can. I hear a thud in the distance. "There's something else I did. Will gave me a book to write my songs in. Inside the cover, he wrote an inscription. It was like a poem. Anyway, some guy at school took it from me, read it aloud, started calling me a queer. I punched him in the stomach, and afterward I threw the book in the trash." I pick up another rock and throw it. "I've been calling my father a hypocrite, and now look at me."

"Noah, you made a mistake, but you're not a hypocrite."

"Yeah, well, I'm not so sure. Anyway, thanks for coming here with me," I say. "Thanks for listening. And I really *am* sorry about the song."

She shakes her head. "Don't be. I'm beginning to understand it better now. Come on, let's get out of here."

We hike to the twin falls and take seats, side by side, atop the flat limestone bedrock. It's a warm day. Aubrey kicks off her shoes and puts her feet in the water. I run my hand over Will's book again. There's a lump in my throat. "Aubrey? There's one last thing I need to tell you. Actually, there's something I need to *show* you. But before I do, would you promise me . . ." I can barely get the words out.

"What? Noah? Promise what?"

"It's just . . . I don't want you to think I'm crazy. Carson

167

already does, and half the time I think he's right. Anyway, here." I pull Will's book from my pocket. "This was Will's. He wrote poems and lyrics in it, some other stuff too. I found it near his body, tossed aside in a pile of leaves. I didn't give it to the police as evidence. I lied, said I didn't find anything."

"Whoa. That's not good."

"No, but right now, that's the least of my worries. You see, I found other things in this book—poems—but I don't think Will wrote them. I think they're clues."

"Clues?"

"To the murders."

Her eyes widen. "Show me."

I scoot a little closer to Aubrey and open the book. After she reads "Potter's Field," I tell her about Hawk's note, the John eight Bible passage, and the cemetery phone number. "And the freaky thing is," I say, "it's all written on the page from the day I met Will, the day I sang that Lead Belly song for him and he wrote it down."

"Wow, that's odd."

"No kidding."

Next I turn to the entry dated September ninth and show her the poem "For Kyle." "Will wrote that poem right after Kyle died," I say, "but look here, in the margin. There's something else."

Aubrey takes the book. I watch her lips move as she silently reads "One Small Act of Kindness." She looks up. "Noah, this is scary."

"So you believe me?"

"Why wouldn't I?"

"Okay, good. And you don't think I'm crazy?"

"No, of course not. But tell me, is there anything else in here? Are there any other clues?"

"I don't know. I was afraid to look." I'd be embarrassed to admit this to any other girl. But not Aubrey.

She stares at me for a while, then lifts her feet from the water, scoots back, and sits cross-legged. Little puddles form on the rock in front of us. She starts flipping through the pages. "All right. Think back, Noah. Try to remember. What day did the police find Paul Mateo's body?"

I don't have to think at all. If I'd had the guts, that's what I would have looked at next. But I didn't. "It was a Monday," I say. "October eleventh."

Aubrey turns a few more pages. "Here it is. There's a poem with no title." She reads:

> *"So much depends upon*
> *a white boy,*
> *singing a slave song on the dirty steps,*
> *eyes closed, strumming steel,*
> *a lost soul, like me."*

She looks up. "Noah, what is it? What's wrong?"

"That's . . . well, a poem Will wrote about me. *I'm* the boy on the steps, singing the song. It's about the day Will and I met on the Drag. He wrote the poem on October eleventh, which is the same day the police found Paul's body."

"It's a good poem," Aubrey says, biting her lip.

"I know. But, Aubrey, is there anything else on that page?"

Slowly, she looks down and runs her finger along the margin. A few seconds later, her eyes meet mine. "There is."

I lean over and take a look. I see another poem in the light, shaky handwriting.

Playing God

Are some lives worth more than others?
Is death more satisfying when it comes
to the least of our brothers?
Victim number two had no soul,
but turn the page and you'll see,
victim number three was gold.

"Noah? What does it mean?"

I read it over again. "Victim number two must be Paul Mateo. Will knew him when they were younger. He told me that Paul got teased a lot—kids called him faggot and queer. Will felt bad because he never stood up for Paul. Anyway, they lost touch, but Will found out that Paul had been hustling on the streets right before he was murdered."

"That's so sad," Aubrey says. "I can't believe kids, right here in Austin, live that way." She glances down at the poem. "Noah, what about . . ."

"Number three? That must be Will. Gold."

"The poem says to turn the page," Aubrey says.

"Right. Go ahead."

I follow along as Aubrey reads aloud.

"Gold

The greater the sacrifice,
The greater the reward.
Number three, slain with a kiss,
The others, a sword.

"How weird. Number three, slain with a kiss? Do you think he's referring to the way Judas Iscariot betrayed Jesus with a kiss?"

"I don't know. Maybe. This guy is so twisted." I think about everything Quindlan told me—about the less-dead, about the killer's wanting to rid society of evil, and about how he preys on gay foster boys. "He must believe he's on a mission from God. But *which* god, I don't know."

Aubrey reads the poem one more time. "Noah, what day did Will die?"

"October twenty-third."

My heart drums as Aubrey flips through the pages. She reads silently for a moment. "This doesn't make sense," she says. "The last entry is dated November tenth. That's ten days from now."

I lean over and take a look.

Number Four

This one's tricky
and requires some thought.
Pay attention,
look around you.
The answer
will be taught.

"Will be *taught*? What does that mean?" I say.

"I don't know," Aubrey says. "This one's more like a riddle. Maybe it means you'll get more clues."

"So it's not over yet. And if everything ties together, it means there could be another murder on November tenth. Oh, God. Aubrey, I'm really starting to think I should show this book to the police."

Aubrey looks at me. "I'm scared, Noah. What will they do when they find out you lied?"

"Arrest me, I guess."

"Is there any other way?"

"I don't know. I still have some time. It could be risky, but there might be someone I can talk to."

{twenty}

I FIND Hawk at school the next day. He's in the boys' locker room, talking to one of the jocks I recognize from McCallum—the one who got expelled for selling his prescription meds for ADD. "I need to talk to you," I say. "It's important."

Hawk nods, motions for the jock to leave, then leads me to an empty row of lockers. "Noah, hey, what's going on?"

"I need to show you something." I know this is a risk, but if Will trusted Hawk, then maybe I can too. Maybe Quindlan is wrong. I reach into my pocket and pull out Will's book.

"Oh my God. Where did you get that?"

"The morning I found Will's body, I found this, too, in a pile of leaves. I know it was a stupid thing to do, but I didn't hand it over to the police. They asked if I'd found anything else. I said no. I kept it."

Hawk stares at me. "Yeah, that *was* stupid. It's called

tampering with evidence. You could have been arrested, Noah."

"I know that."

"Wait. Didn't you tell me that Will accidentally left that book at the campsite, and went back to get it?"

"Yeah. That's what Quindlan told me. It was the night me and Carson played at the Red Room. Supposedly Will went to find the book right before our show."

"And he never came back," Hawk says. "So the killer must have followed him there." He thinks this over for a moment. "Anyway, why are you telling me this? And why are you showing *me* the book?"

"Because I wanted you to look at a few things written inside. Besides Quindlan and Doomsday, you're the only person I know who was friends with Will. And this is going to sound really weird, but I found some poems in here—ones Will didn't write—and I think they might be clues. To all three of the murders."

"Are you serious?"

"I wish I wasn't, but yeah. I thought maybe you could help me understand."

Hawk glances around nervously. "The bell's going to ring soon. Meet me after school in the parking lot. We'll go for a drive. I'll take a look."

† † †

"Noah, why *didn't* you turn this book in to the police? What was your reason?"

Hawk is flipping through Will's book for the third time.

174

We're sitting in his car—an old Mustang convertible—parked on an empty side street far from campus. When we first arrived, I told him everything, and he studied each clue in the book for a long time. He even took out a pen and paper and jotted things down.

"I don't know. Part of me just wanted to keep it, and part of me was really angry. Will told me he wore a wire for the police after he got busted for dealing. The police used him. And when he needed their help, they weren't there for him."

"Whoa. Hold on. Will told you about wearing the wire?"

"Yeah."

Hawk studies me. "Wearing that wire kept him out of jail. Will was seventeen when he got busted. He wouldn't have gone to juvie. He would have gone to an adult prison."

"Yeah, well, a lot of good that does him now," I say. "Besides, I'm surprised *you*, of all people, are defending the police."

Hawk shrugs. He looks tired; his Mohawk is limp and his nose bolt is red and infected. "I'm not defending them. Let's just say I've been around the block a few times. I've had to do plenty of risky things. Anyway"—he taps the book—"I think you've got something here. But do you really believe the killer wrote the poems, the clues, for *you*? I mean, that's pretty far out, Noah."

I sigh. "I know it sounds insane, even paranoid, but think about it. The first clue was written on the page from the day I met Will, in the margin next to the Lead Belly song. The second clue was written on the page from the day Kyle was murdered, the third on the day Paul was killed, right beside the poem Will wrote about *me*. I guess it could

175

be a coincidence, but it doesn't feel that way. It feels personal."

"So if you're right, the killer knows you. Kept his eye on you and Will when you were together."

"Yeah. Exactly. It's pretty creepy."

"And if all of this is true, the killer would have written these clues in the book right after he strangled Will."

"Right," I say. "Which goes along with the autopsy report. Supposedly there were several hours between the time Will died and the time the cross was carved into his chest. He could have written in Will's book during that time."

Hawk gives me a strange look. "Wait a minute. How do you know about the autopsy report? It wasn't released to the public."

I swallow hard. "Oh, right, well . . ."

"Noah, who've you been talking to?"

"I can't tell you that. I'm sorry."

"Listen, just sit on this for a while. Don't do anything. We have some time. I'm going to talk to some people I know. Get a few things straight."

"Like who? Who would you talk to?"

"I can't tell you that." Hawk opens the book and jots down a few more things. "I've got all the information I need. I want you to promise me that you won't go to the police. At this point, they could screw up everything. If what you say is true, then it really does look like there's going to be another murder. And if your theory's right, November tenth would be the day. I may have a way to prevent it. Trust me, okay?"

I look into his eyes, remembering Quindlan's warning. I can only hope I'm doing the right thing.

"And if you hear anything else, or if someone contacts you, let me know. Here's my number." Hawk rips off a piece of paper, writes down his number, and hands it to me. "Come on. That's enough for today. I'll take you home."

† † †

I say goodbye to Hawk and watch his Mustang disappear around the corner. A second later, Melanie runs outside. "Noah, I'm scared. It's Daddy. He's in the kitchen. He's really upset. He's been on the phone with the police."

"The police?"

I run into the kitchen. My father is sitting at the table with his head in his hands. "Dad? What's going on?"

He looks up. "Noah. Thank goodness you're home. I was getting worried. He called today."

"What do you mean? Who?"

"The *caller*. On my show. I recognized his voice right away. I phoned the police, but again they weren't able to trace him."

"What did he say?"

"Well, it was strange. It wasn't his usual ranting about Austin's gay community. Instead, he asked me a very unusual question. One I'd never heard on my show before. It was about the woman caught in adultery—you know, from the Gospel of John? He wanted to know what I thought Jesus wrote in the sand."

My legs feel weak. I pull out a chair and take a seat next to my father. "How did you answer him?"

"I told him I didn't know, that I needed to think it over.

177

Actually, I was stalling for time. I thought the police might be able to trace him, but they couldn't. Anyway, I asked him to call back tomorrow. The police said they'll be waiting."

Later that night, while I'm lying in bed, unable to sleep, I consider calling Hawk. I even consider calling Quindlan. But instead, I pick up the phone and dial Aubrey's number.

"Noah? What's going on? It's late. Are you okay?"

"Yeah. I need to go somewhere tomorrow. I was wondering if you'd come with me."

{twenty-one}

THE FOLLOWING morning, I meet Aubrey on the corner near her house. "Aubrey, before we go, I need to ask you something. And it has nothing to do with Will or the murders or any of this. It's about you and Brandon. Are the two of you together? I just need to know."

Aubrey sighs and glances down at the pavement. She unhitches her book bag from her shoulder and lets it fall to the ground. "Yes . . . well, *no*. I mean, I thought we were, until . . ." She trails off.

"Until what?"

"I know this sounds crazy, Noah, but until you sang that song for me at the Red Room."

"The song? Aubrey, can you explain that? I'm a little confused."

"I was too, until I figured it out. You see, after you sang those lyrics, I was really mad, only I realized later I wasn't angry with you. I was angry with *me*."

"Really?" I raise an eyebrow and playfully rub the side of my face where she smacked me that night.

"I'm sorry, Noah." She reaches up and gently touches my face. Her hand is warm; it feels nice. "I was an idiot. I shouldn't have done that. It's just—"

"No, it's okay. Actually, the crowd loved it. Responded very well to the violence. You should have seen it; they went wild. But I'm still confused. Why are you angry with yourself?"

"Because I didn't even realize what happened between us that day, you know, in the woods, at that stupid youth retreat."

"And what happened?" I ask, biting my lip. I'm not sure I want to hear the answer.

"A *lot*. But I got scared, Noah. I didn't know what to do. We'd been friends for so long. And with all the trouble you'd been getting into, getting kicked out of school, all the heat from my parents, I was so mixed up." Aubrey looks up shyly. Her eyes meet mine.

"Well, how about for now we go back to being friends?" I say. "It would be a start."

She smiles. "Yeah, I'd like that."

"Me too."

Together we hop the bus heading downtown and get off outside KMBJ. Aubrey's dad has no clue that she just cut school to do a little sleuthing with Satan's spawn, and my father has no idea that I'm about to be a guest speaker on his show.

We walk past the radio tower and satellite dishes. Inside the building, we say hi to the receptionist, who flashes us a big smile and tells me how much I've grown. It's been years since I've visited. We pass the production room, where a bunch of Bible zealots are working, and peek inside my dad's studio. He's alone, drinking coffee and fiddling with some knobs on the console. It's funny: when I was a kid, I used to love to come here. My father would sit me on his lap and let me talk into the microphone, play with all the gizmos. That was when I thought he was the infallible mouth of God, before I figured out he was more like the guy behind the curtain in *The Wizard of Oz*, pulling levers, pushing buttons, projecting an all-powerful image across the airwaves.

We open the door and walk in. "Noah? Aubrey?" he says, looking startled. "What are you doing here? Why aren't you in school?"

Aubrey and I timed it just right. It's three minutes before showtime. My dad's headgear is on. The phone lines are already blinking. No time for explanations. "It's okay, Dad," I say. "I want to be here when he calls."

Worriedly, he glances at the clock and takes a look at the computer screen. "Well, you're in luck. I believe that's him." He points to the word *private* blinking in red on the monitor. "He's already on line three, waiting."

Aubrey and I take seats against the wall while my dad contacts the police. "Yes, Officer, I'm pretty sure it's him," he says. "We'll be recording the show. Thank you."

My dad spins a few dials and plays a quick commercial advertising a Christian weight-loss program. After a lady sings a jingle—*"Three scriptures a day keep those unwanted pounds at bay"*—my father clears his throat and leans into the microphone. "Hello, friends. Good morning, and God bless you. This is the Bible Answer Guy, John Nordstrom, broadcasting from Austin, Texas. . . ."

Aubrey whispers in my ear, "Noah, do you know what you're going to say to the guy?"

"No. I figure I can wing it."

My father takes the calls in order, but I can barely focus on the first two questions. There's a crazy lady convinced that the new chip implants are the Mark of the Beast, and next is a guy who's freaking out about his yoga-loving son who, instead of meditating on the Word of God, meditates on the word *om*.

My dad gives both callers his typical evangelical answers. He explains the various interpretations of the number 666, then goes on to talk about the differences between Christianity and Eastern religions and tells caller number two to pray for his son to find the truth. After each call, he quotes from first Timothy, "For God did not give us a spirit of fear, but of power, love, and a sound mind." And even though I'm not about to jump on the Bible Answer Guy bandwagon, I think that verse makes a lot of sense. Especially the part about the sound mind.

When my father is finally ready to take caller number three, he turns to me and nods.

"Hello. John Nordstrom here. I'm ready for your question."

"Well, hello again, Dr. Nordstrom. We spoke yesterday. Do you remember?"

"Ah, yes, of course. The mystery man. So, your question was, what did Jesus write in the sand?"

As my father is speaking, I slip him a note. It reads *When you're finished, let me talk to him. Please.*

Our eyes meet. He hesitates for a moment, then leans toward the microphone. "I'm sorry to say that I haven't been able to come up with an answer yet. You see, the Lord's been dealing with me lately. It seems I think I know more than I do, which has been quite a humbling experience"—he chuckles—"seeing that I'm the Bible Answer Guy. Anyway, I must admit, I'm stumped by your question, but my son, Noah, is here in the studio, and he has some interesting insights. I think you'll enjoy speaking with him. Noah?"

I look at my dad, wondering if he really meant what he said about the Lord dealing with him, or if he's just playing a game with the caller. He hands me a headset. I put it on. All of a sudden, I realize that not only are thousands of people listening to this show, but several police officers as well, and I have no idea how I'm going to pull this off.

"Um, hi," I say. The workers from the production room appear outside the studio window with their jaws hanging open. My dad has never had a live guest on his show before. One of the Bible zealots taps on the window. My dad flashes him a thumbs-up.

"Why, I'm totally honored," the caller says. "Imagine, to be speaking with the Bible Answer Guy's son. Tell me, Noah, are you planning on following in your father's footsteps?"

It seems the caller is playing a game too. There's a hint of sarcasm in his voice, and he seems to be challenging me. "Um, no, actually. Not at all. You may be surprised by this, but I don't have much use for religion. Or church, for that matter." I glance at my dad. I expect him to have a disapproving look on his face, but he doesn't. However, the Bible zealots lined up at the window are freaking out. I ignore them. "I do believe in God, though, but my father and I have different views on a lot of subjects, especially on how to interpret the Bible. He's much more literal than I am."

Now there's a faint smile on my father's face.

"Really?" the caller says. "That's very interesting. I must admit, I side with your father. I'm a literalist, a black-and-white kind of guy. What the Bible says, I believe is fact and not open to interpretation. But I'm interested to hear your opinion. So, tell me, Noah, what do you think Jesus wrote in the sand?"

"A poem," I say.

"A poem?" He chuckles. "Well, I didn't know Jesus was a poet."

"Oh, he was. Absolutely. I mean, he was with God in the beginning, so he created the world, right? And whether you believe it was in six days or six hundred million years, that's still poetry."

"Yes, I suppose that's true."

"He also inspired the Psalms of King David, and the love songs of King Solomon," I add. "He spoke in parables, too, which all have hidden meanings. In fact, the Bible tells us that Jesus never spoke *without* using a parable. So I believe there was a hidden meaning in what he wrote in the sand. Clues, maybe, to a future event."

"Oh. You mean, like a prediction of his *death*, possibly?"

I glance at Aubrey. Her eyes are wide.

"Yes," I say. "His death. That's quite possible, seeing that Jesus came to earth with a specific mission: to die."

The line is quiet for a while. "So," he says, "Jesus may have written something like this. The place: Golgotha. The time: the sixth hour. The method: crucifixion. The betrayal: a kiss."

For a moment I can't speak. I'm trying to process everything he said, see if it makes sense. Meanwhile Aubrey whispers something in my dad's ear. He nods, pushes a few buttons on the computer, and hands me a phone. He whispers, "Here. I'll take the next call. See if you can talk to him off the air."

I take off my headset and hand it to my father. He pushes a few more buttons and says, "Thank you, Noah, for being our special guest. And thank you, mystery man, for your very intriguing question. And now, may I take the next caller?"

I walk a few paces and put the phone to my ear. "Who are you?" I demand. "What do you want? Why are you doing this?"

At first all I hear is breathing. Then a laugh. "I'm impressed, Noah. You're a smart boy. Brave, too. Keep searching for the truth. You're definitely on the right path. And remember this: Jesus was betrayed by a friend."

"Wait, I—"

Suddenly he hangs up, and all that's left is a dial tone.

{twenty-two}

"THAT'S IT?" Aubrey says. "That's all you're going to do?"

Detective Adams nods. "I'm sorry. That's all we *can* do."

We're still at my dad's studio. Adams, one of the detectives working on the case, showed up fifteen minutes after the show. "We'll continue looking into the possibilities, Dr. Nordstrom," he says, "but right now we don't have a solid reason to believe this caller is also the killer. It appears to be a coincidence that he called a week before Kyle Lester was murdered, and had some negative things to say about the gay community. Today he didn't mention anything along those lines. However, it looks like he dialed from a pay phone, so we'll check out the location, and see if we can get some prints."

"Yes, thank you, I understand," my father says.

"And if you get prints?" I say. My heart is still pounding in my chest. Even if the police get prints, I know what I have to do.

"We'll keep you informed," he says. "Please, all of you, rest assured, the police are working very hard on this case. Dr. Nordstrom, thank you for alerting us about the caller. We'll keep our eyes and ears open. We'll let you know if there are any further developments."

† † †

The next day, I turn on my cell phone and punch in Quindlan's number. Right now I don't care what Hawk said about not contacting the police. And if Quindlan slaps a set of handcuffs on me, well, I'll just have to deal with it.

Quindlan answers on the first ring. "Hi, Noah. What's up?"

"Hey. We need to talk. And I need to show you something. It's important."

"All right. I'm hanging out with Doomsday at our usual spot on the Drag. Hold on a second." I hear shuffling and a dog barking. Quindlan whispers, "Remember, don't say or do anything to blow my cover around Doomsday. In fact, why don't you play the Good Samaritan and take this poor homeless guy out for lunch? I'm starved."

"How does the Thai Noodle House sound?" I say.

"Great."

Thirty minutes later, Carson and I park the DPCP's old Lexus and cross Guadalupe on foot. "I can't believe you're making me do this," Carson says.

"I told you, I need a decoy. I need you to hang out with Doomsday while I talk to Quindlan alone."

"But Doomsday's crazy. And I think he hates me.

Remember the way he was preaching at me last time? 'If your right eye causes you to sin, pluck it out. Better to lose one eye than to be thrown into hell.'"

"Just tell him you repented and you're getting baptized. He'll love that. The two of you should have a lot to talk about."

Carson stops. "Noah, wait." There's a serious look on his face. "What about you? Are you sure you want to go through with this? I mean, you could toss that book in the trash right now. Go home. Forget the whole thing."

"No, I can't do that."

"God, I wish you had listened to me in the first place and burned that damn book."

"Yeah, well, I didn't. And I'm doing this for Will. Plus, if some other kid gets killed because I didn't do the right thing, then I won't be able to live with myself. So just do me a favor, okay? If Quindlan arrests me, go home and tell my parents. Tell them *everything*. And give Aubrey a call too."

"Right. And we'll make sure to visit you in jail. I can't believe you're doing this."

As we approach, Hercules barks and barrels toward Carson. "Whoa, hey, Hercules." Carson bends down and scratches the dog behind his ears while Hercules jumps up and licks his face.

"What do you know? We've got company, Dooms," Quindlan says. He sits up on his bedroll, yawns, and stretches.

Doomsday is leaning against the church door, smoking a cigarette and reading a collection of poems by Pablo Neruda. When he sees me, his eyes widen. Guiltily, he drops his cigarette and stomps on it. "Oh, my. Sorry. Filthy habit. Hello, Noah. Did you come back to discuss end-time prophecy? I certainly hope so."

"No, I didn't. Actually, I need to talk to Quindlan. And Carson wants to hang out with you for a while."

Doomsday's eyes narrow at Carson. "Is that so?"

"Um, yeah," Carson says. "You see, I'm getting baptized soon, and I could use some advice."

A smile spreads across Doomsday's face. He sets down his book. "When one sinner repents, all the angels in heaven rejoice! Come, tell me all about it. Will you have sprinkling or full immersion?"

Carson shoots me a look. "Well, I'll be getting dunked in my girlfriend's pool, so I guess you'd call that full immersion."

"Wonderful. The best method."

I give Carson a little push toward Doomsday. "Go ahead, dude," I whisper. "And say a prayer for me. I'm gonna need it."

As Quindlan and I walk down the church steps, Doomsday calls out, "Watch out for Mr. Quindlan, Noah. He's a maniac."

Quindlan laughs. "Okay, Dooms. Whatever you say."

† † †

Inside the Thai restaurant, Quindlan shovels a forkful of noodles into his mouth and turns a page in Will's book. I've dog-eared all the pages with poems written by the killer, and Quindlan is studying each one. There's a plate of spicy, steaming noodles in front of me, but I can't eat. "So, what do you think?" I say.

"Well, this is certainly an interesting piece of evidence. Apparently the killer is quite intelligent. Very organized. Not a bad poet, either. And for whatever reason, he wanted you, or *someone*, to find this book."

I wait for Quindlan to read me my Miranda rights, but he doesn't. Instead, he says, "Noah, I'd like to keep this. I'll show it to the detectives working on the case. I'm sure the profiler will be thrilled to have it."

I stare at him in disbelief. "Um, yeah, of course. That's why I came here. To give you the book."

"Great." He sets it on the table and motions toward my plate. "Now, please, eat. Your food's getting cold."

"That's it?" I say. "You're not going to charge me with anything?"

"Why would I do that?"

"Well, because I tampered with evidence. I found the book at Will's campsite and didn't turn it over to the police. Plus, I lied."

"Well, yes, that's true. You should have given the book to the police right from the start, but honestly, I don't blame you for taking it. If I was in your position, young and stupid, I probably would have done the same thing. Will was your friend. The book was something he probably would have wanted you to have. You didn't know it would contain clues to the murders."

All of a sudden I realize I've been holding my breath for a long time. I let it out and suck in more air. "But what will you tell the other detectives? How will you explain it all?"

"That's my business, Noah. Don't worry about it. The important thing is that we have the book now. And we're closer than ever to solving the case. Please, eat."

It feels like a huge weight has been lifted off my shoulders. "Gosh, I don't know what to say, except, well, *thank you*."

"No problem. You were smart to come to me."

I feel my whole body relax. Suddenly I'm hungry. The noodles are still warm. I eat a forkful and take more. When I've finished half my plate, I say, "Quindlan, can I ask you something?"

He's still eating his lunch and flipping through the book. He looks up. "Sure."

"Last time we spoke, you told me the police believed that Warren Banks killed Kyle and Paul, and that someone else, maybe from the Westboro church, killed Will. But don't the clues in the book point to *one* killer?"

He nods. "Yes, I believe so."

"Okay, well, I didn't mention this before, but last week my father and I visited Warren Banks in prison. Banks told us that he was with Kyle the night he was killed, but Kyle left with someone else—a guy asking for spare change. A guy who was also carrying a *Bible*. And then yesterday I went to my father's studio, and—"

Quindlan holds up one hand. "I know. I heard the show. I took a little time off last night, went to my apartment, and listened to the Internet broadcast. I thought you were very good, Noah."

"So that means you heard the question the caller asked? About the woman caught in adultery, and what Jesus wrote in the sand?"

191

"I did."

"And didn't that freak you out? I mean, you said that was Will's favorite Bible passage, and that Doomsday chose it for the chaplain to read at his burial."

Quindlan nods. "Yes, it was alarming."

"Do you think it's possible . . . ?"

He looks at me. "That Doomsday is the killer? No, I don't. But it could be someone else who was close to Will."

I hesitate for a moment. "Hawk?"

Quindlan doesn't answer. He sets down his fork and takes out paper and a pen. He begins to write, and when he's done, he hands the paper to me. It reads:

Golgotha
The 6th hour
Crucifixion
Kiss

The words the caller used. What he suggested Jesus might have written in the sand. A prediction of Jesus's death. Clues to a future event.

"I suppose we could make several guesses as to who killed Will, but here's what I think," Quindlan says. "If our theory is right, those must be the final clues. There's an abandoned warehouse on the east side, about five miles off Manor Road. It's marked with a huge skull and crossbones spray-painted on the outside wall. Not too long ago I busted a bunch of guys cooking batches of meth out there. I found out the dealers called the warehouse Golgotha, which means 'place of the skull.'"

"And Golgotha was the name of the hill where Jesus was crucified," I say. "So you think that's where the next murder might take place? Inside that warehouse?"

"It's possible."

"And the sixth hour," I say. "That was the time Jesus died."

"Right. According to the Aramaic calendar, that would be three in the afternoon our time."

"I guess that makes sense, but"—I glance at the list—"what about crucifixion? That's crazy. I mean how—"

"Not so crazy, Noah. When the Romans crucified their prisoners, do you know how they actually died?"

I think this over for a moment. "Yes, I do," I say, remembering one of Pastor Simpson's sermons. "They died by asphyxiation."

"Exactly." Quindlan spreads out his arms like he's on a cross. "After they were beaten, bloodied, nailed, and left hanging for a while, they just didn't have the strength to breathe. So instead of a cross, our guy uses a rope." He drops his hands. "You might say he crucifies his victims in a more civilized way."

"Oh, God. And what about the word *kiss*?"

"Hmmm. That's the one that really troubles me. The one that makes me believe the killer is a friend of Will's."

My heart begins to pound. "Quindlan? The caller said something to me off the air. He said, 'Remember this: Jesus was betrayed by a friend.'"

Quindlan nods slowly. "Noah, it's important for you to realize that for you, this is over. You don't need to be involved anymore. You've done all you can, and now you need to move on. Look, I know you didn't get to resolve things with Will, but you can't dwell on it. It's over. Think about other interests: school, your friends, your music—and what about Aubrey? Did things work out with you and her?"

"Yeah. Sort of."

"Good. Spend time with her. Hang out with your friends. Try not to think about any of this. I'll be there, at the warehouse, on November tenth. I promise. And I'll have a team of officers with me. A big backup crew. If all of this is true, we'll get the guy. The murders will end. There's no need for you to worry anymore."

"Okay." I turn the paper over, slide it to Quindlan, and hand him the pen. "But will you do one thing for me? Draw me a map to Golgotha?"

"Noah, you can't go there. It's dangerous."

"I just want to drive by. Today, in broad daylight, before I go home. I just need to see the place with my own eyes. It'll help me put everything to rest."

Reluctantly, Quindlan takes the pen from my hand. He taps it against the table a few times, then begins to draw.

He hands me the map. "Don't do anything foolish, Noah."

† † †

"There it is," I say. "There's the warehouse. I see the skull."

Carson parks the Lexus on the side of the road. We're in

no-man's-land, a big barren field in the middle of nowhere. The eye sockets of the spray-painted skull seem to be staring directly at me.

"So that's Golgotha?" Carson says.

"That's it." We sit there for a while, staring at the building. A farm truck carrying huge bales of hay passes by. Cows are mooing in the distance. "Come on, let's go inside and check it out," I say.

"What? Are you crazy? Going inside wasn't part of the deal, Noah. I said I'd drive by. That's all. Quindlan gave you a get-out-of-jail-free card. If you were smart, you'd take it and run."

I open the car door. "Fine. I'll go alone, then."

"No! Wait!" Carson gets out. "You're not going alone. Just . . . hold on." He heads to the back of the car and opens the trunk. "Here, take one of these." He tosses me one of the DPCP's prosthetic legs and takes one for himself. "If we're going in, we'll need weapons. Good thing I didn't drop these off at the factory yet."

I grip the leg. It's as heavy as a baseball bat. "Good thinking, dude."

We walk across the field. The air is still. It's deathly quiet.

I try several doors before I find one that's unlocked. "Carson, come here. This one's open." Slowly, we walk inside. It's dark and musty. Carson walks through a huge spiderweb. "Gross." He spits and sputters. A rat scurries across the floor.

"Okay, are you happy? Can we go now?" Carson says. "There's nothing in here. It's just an old, empty warehouse."

"Wait." I open a dirty window and sunlight pours in. As my eyes adjust, I begin to see words spray-painted on the wall. "Carson, look over there." Several lines are written in bold red letters. "Oh my God. It's another poem," I say.

Carson stares and reads aloud.

> **"Number Four**
> *Your sin spreads like cancer,*
> *rots the bones.*
> *Slides like water*
> *over stones.*
> *Permeates.*
> *Regurgitates.*
> *Infuriates.*
> *Is your life worth more,*
> *number four?*
> *Does God keep score?"*

Suddenly a face appears in the open window. An old guy wearing a straw hat. "Hey! Who's in there? Goddamn you kids!"

"Oh my God. Carson, run!"

The two of us bolt through the open door and race to the car. The guy calls after us, "You got no business here! Stay away!"

We jump in; Carson starts the engine and we take off. I toss my limb into the backseat. "Whoa, dude, that was close."

"Yeah, no kidding."

"Hey, where's your leg?" I say.

"I don't know. I must have dropped it."

We drive a mile or so and come to a red light. Carson stops and turns to me. "Noah, what does the poem mean?"

I close my eyes and run through the lines in my head. "I'm not sure, but I think the killer is about to break his mold."

{twenty-three}

"DO YOU know where Quindlan is?"

It's November tenth. I'm at school, in the cafeteria, sitting at a lunch table, staring at my plate of pork and beans. I spin around and see Hawk. "Quindlan? No."

"When was the last time you saw him?" he whispers fiercely.

"Last week. On the Drag. Why?"

"It doesn't matter *why*. I need to find him. Now."

I haven't seen Hawk since the day he took me for a ride in his Mustang and I showed him Will's book. "And what about *you*?" I say. "Where have you been? You said you were going to talk to some people about the stuff in Will's book. You told me I could trust you. But how can I when all you do is disappear?"

"Look, Noah, I don't have time to explain. Just *think*. Do you have *any* idea where Quindlan could be?"

I look into Hawk's eyes. They're like cold steel. If he's

the killer, he'll go to Golgotha today. Quindlan will be there waiting. He'll fall into his trap. "No. I don't."

Hawk tries to stare me down one last time. Then he turns around and stalks out of the cafeteria. The door slams and my stomach lurches.

Two hours later, as I'm sitting in pre-cal, staring at the clock, I realize I have to do something. I can't just sit and watch the minutes tick by until three p.m. The sixth hour. The next murder. I grab my books, stand up, and march out of the classroom. The security guard tries to stop me, but I run past him, race down the hall, and dart into Mr. Dobbs's room. "I need to use your phone," I say. "Please, it's an emergency."

He nods and motions toward the phone on the wall. "Sure, Noah, go ahead."

I pick up the receiver and dial Quindlan's cell. He answers on the first ring. "Hello. Who's this?"

"Quindlan, it's me, Noah. I need to—"

"Noah! I'm glad you called. Listen, I need you to come here right away. To the warehouse. Golgotha. I have the guy. The killer. He's about to confess, but he says he wants to talk to *you* first. He insists on finishing the conversation he had with you on your father's radio show."

"He wants to talk to *me?*"

"Yes. Can you get out of school now? I hate to involve you, Noah, but we need a confession in order to lock him up. Otherwise he might be out on the streets soon again. Do you remember how to get here? Do you still have the map I drew?"

"Yeah, I've got it."

"Okay. Don't say a word about this to anyone. And come alone. It's safe. The police are hiding out around the building. I'll let them know you're coming. Use the front door. It's unlocked. I'm right inside."

"Okay, I'll be there as soon as I can." I hang up. My heart is pounding.

"Noah? Is everything all right?" Mr. Dobbs asks.

"Oh, yeah, everything's fine. Thanks."

I have to get out of here. My only problem is getting past security. But wait. There's a back door I can try. Carson told me that sometimes the janitor accidentally leaves it unlocked. I run out of the classroom. Find the door. Glance around the hall to make sure no one's watching, and give a push. It opens.

I jog quickly to the avenue, hop a city bus that leaves me half a mile from my house, and run home. Thank goodness, no one's there. Our van is in the driveway, and the keys are on the kitchen counter. I grab them, jump in, turn on the engine, and head for Golgotha.

When I arrive, I park the van and look around. Strangely, the place looks exactly the same. No cars, no people. Completely deserted.

My legs feel weak and heavy as I walk toward the warehouse. In less than a minute, I'll be looking into the killer's eyes, talking with him face to face. I turn the handle on the front door. It's unlocked, just like Quindlan said it would be.

"Hello? Quindlan? It's me, Noah."

No answer. I stand there, my heart thumping, while my eyes adjust to the dim light. Two chairs are set up in the corner. The window is boarded shut. The poem on the wall is still there, the words red and ominous.

"Quindlan? Where are you?"

Still no answer. Near the chairs, on the floor, is a pile of newspapers. Beside the pile, a sheet of paper. Slowly, I walk over, bend down, and pick it up. Pasted onto the note are letters cut from newspaper.

WOE to you, who pitched his tent AMONG the sodomites. WhAt A MAN reAps, he wILL sow. ALL thInGs BY LAw Are purGed wIth BLOOd. WIthOut the shedding OF BLOOd there Is nO reMIssIOn.

My hands are shaking. I drop the paper. There's a white bedsheet spread out beside the newspapers. On top of it, a coiled rope. Next to the rope, a glinting piece of metal. I peer more closely and see the sharp blade. A scalpel.

Suddenly I hear the bolt on the door turn and lock into place. I spin around.

"Are you ready to finish our conversation, Noah?"

The voice is the caller's, but the person standing by the door is someone I recognize. It's Quindlan. He's wearing latex gloves, and he's talking into a black box—some kind of electronic device.

I want to scream, but my throat closes up. Run, but my legs won't move. "What's going on?" I manage to choke out. "Is this some kind of joke?"

Quindlan laughs. "Joke? No." He holds up the box. "This is what I used to disguise my voice when I called in to your father's show."

"*You're* the caller?"

"That's right." He motions toward the paper on the ground. "I see you've read my note. Come, have a seat. The two of us have a lot to talk about."

I stare at him. "You're the one? The one who killed Will? And Paul and Kyle?"

"Like I said, Noah, we need to talk."

"No, we don't. Where are the police? You told me the police would be here. You were lying! Let me out!" My eyes dart around as I look for a way out. There isn't one. I run to the side of the building and bang on the wall. "Help! Someone, help!"

Quindlan pulls out a gun. "Don't even think about it, Noah." His thumb slides over the hammer, and I hear a click. He points the gun at me. "If you try to escape, I'll shoot you. And if you scream again, I'll shoot you too. Immediately. That's a promise. Now, take a seat."

Somehow I manage to put one foot in front of the other. I walk to a chair and sit down. As I do, I see a foot poking out from under the pile of newspapers. It freaks me out at first. Is it another one of Quindlan's victims? But then I realize it's the prosthetic leg Carson dropped when we came here last week.

Quindlan follows and takes the seat across from me. "Do you believe in signs, Noah? Visions from God?"

"No, I don't."

"Well, that's a shame. I do. In fact, for the past few years, God's been speaking to me. Do you remember the story I told you about my father? About his ministry, God's Warriors, and how he helped young boys in the South Bronx get off the streets?"

"Yes. I remember. You also said your brother killed himself because your father condemned him for being gay."

"Yes, well, I must admit, I embellished a bit. I never had a brother. I added that small detail to win you over. To make you believe I was sympathetic toward Will. And it worked, didn't it? But you're getting ahead of me, Noah. Let's backtrack a little. There's a part of my story I left out. You see, years ago, when I was sixteen, my father had an idea. He wanted to house some of the boys who'd been addicted to drugs and kicked out of their homes, so he renovated an old apartment building. He even used our family's savings to fund the project. Once the place was up and running, he spent a lot of time there. In fact, after a while, my father rarely came home at night. Like any other kid would, I became angry, jealous. I loved my father. I wanted to know why these street kids were more important to him than me. Than his own family. So I sneaked out of the house one night and went to the apartment building. I found him in bed with one of the boys. There was a gun lying on the dresser in the bedroom. I took it. My hands were shaking but I pointed it right at the boy. My father tried to reason with me. Told me it wasn't what it looked like. Right! He wrestled me to the ground and the gun went off. My father took the bullet in the chest. Killed him instantly."

I look at the gun trembling in Quindlan's hand. "What does this have to do with me? Or with Will, Kyle, or Paul?"

"Everything," Quindlan says.

"No," I say. "Your father did something wrong. Something evil. He took advantage of young boys. Kids who trusted him, looked up to him."

Quindlan nods, but he seems lost in his own thoughts. "A week after my father's death, my mother downed a bottle of pills and never woke up. I was the only one left."

"That's a tragic story," I say. "But it's not a reason for you to kill innocent people."

"Well, they're not exactly innocent, are they, Noah? We both know what the Bible says. Homosexuality is an abomination in God's sight. Punishable by death."

"No. That's not true. You're wrong. People like you use the Bible to justify their own hatred."

"Well, that's why you're next, Noah. Because you've been taught the truth, but you've rejected it." He picks up the note. "In my opinion, you're no better than the others. Their sin is your own. You've pitched your tent in Sodom. Blood must be shed." Quindlan points the gun at my head and keeps an eye on me while he reaches down and grabs the rope. From the corner of my eye, I see the foot of the prosthetic leg. If I can just get Quindlan distracted for a moment, I can jump out of my seat, grab the leg, and swing.

204

But all I can do right now is keep him talking.

"So you're the one who wrote the poems, the clues, in Will's book?" I say.

"Yes. And if you noticed, I was very precise. Each poem was written so that you would see a pattern, Noah. And of course, you figured out that the fourth murder would be today. November tenth. But you needed more clues, so I called in to your father's show. I was thrilled when I was able to speak with you on the air. Everything went according to plan. You even called me today, just like I knew you would. Like I said, God was speaking to me the whole time. He told me a cleansing had to be performed, and I was the one to do it."

"No, that wasn't God," I say. "That was your own sick mind."

"Be careful what you say, Noah. Blasphemy is the unforgivable sin." He fingers the rope. "Now, shall we continue?"

I glance again at the prosthetic leg. "No. I want to know something else. How did you even know I would go to Will's campsite? How did you know I would take his book?"

He shrugs. "That's the beauty of it. I didn't. It was a test. I was testing God to see if you were the next boy to die. Like I said, I'm very precise. Do you know the story of Gideon and the fleece?"

I swallow hard. "Yes, I do. Gideon put out a sheep's fleece on the ground at night. He told God that if the fleece was wet with dew in the morning, and the ground dry, he would obey God's order to kill the enemy."

"Exactly. Will's book was my fleece, Noah. I set it on the ground. When you took it, I knew you were the one. And when you figured out all the clues inside, and when we spoke on the air, well, your sentence was set in stone. Of course, your murder carries a much bigger risk for me. You're not one of the less-dead. A thorough investigation will follow your murder. They won't quit until they find the killer. I know that. But I'm prepared. Actually, I'm looking forward to it. Your murder will be broadcast all over the country. I have many entertaining evenings ahead of me, watching the news while the police try to solve the crime. Your friendship with Will will be perceived as sexual, illicit, I'm sure. And I believe that once people understand the abomination of homosexuality, they will be thankful for the cleansing. Do you believe in fate, Noah?"

"No," I say. "There's no such thing as fate. People make choices. That's what I believe. Like you. You chose to become a police officer, but then you chose to abuse your authority. You're supposed to enforce the law, protect people, but instead you murder innocent boys. That's a choice, not fate."

"Hmmm, choices." Quindlan snaps the rope.

I don't have much time.

I lunge for the prosthetic leg, but Quindlan is fast. He grabs me and turns me around, and I feel the rope dig into my neck. I'm coughing, choking, pulling, kicking. The walls begin to spin.

Suddenly I hear a dog barking. Loud knocking on the warehouse door. "Mr. Quindlan! Mr. Quindlan! Are you in there?"

It's Doomsday. And Hercules.

"Dooms! Not now!" Quindlan yells. "I told you not to come here!" The rope loosens.

It's my only chance. I break free, lunge for the leg, grab it, and swing with all my might. I hear a loud crack, a moan, and a thud. Quindlan falls to the ground. I'm about to run, but next comes an explosion; my ears ring, and the warehouse door flies open. Hawk runs in. And then I realize that Hawk blew the lock off the door with his gun.

"Noah!" he yells. "Hurry, get out! Now!"

I run outside. Doomsday is there, and together we watch from the door. Quindlan is struggling to get up now, but Hawk quickly grabs Quindlan's gun and handcuffs him behind his back. Next thing I know, sirens begin to blare, and there's a swarm of police cars circling the warehouse.

Hercules barrels into the building. He sniffs Quindlan, licks his face, and begins to whine.

Doomsday turns away. He's shaking. "How could he do this? Mr. Quindlan was my friend. My good friend."

Three police officers race past us and into the warehouse. They take over.

"Noah?" Hawk runs over to me. "Hey, are you all right?" He examines my neck and winces.

"Yeah, I'm okay." My voice is hoarse. I can barely speak. It feels like someone has kicked me in the throat.

Doomsday moans. He covers his face with both hands and begins to sob.

"Hey, Dooms, it's going to be all right," Hawk says, putting his arm around him. "Thanks to you, we got here just in time. And look, Noah's going to be fine."

I look at Hawk. "What's going on? How did you know I'd come here?"

Hawk reaches into his pocket and takes out a badge. "I'm a police officer, Noah."

"You?"

A loud siren wails and an ambulance pulls up in front of the warehouse. "Yes. Now come on. Let's get you to the hospital."

{twenty-four}

"SO YOU'RE the undercover cop who arrested Will? Asked him to wear the wire?"

Hawk and I are sitting in my hospital room. He's in a chair and I'm propped up in bed, wearing one of those pathetic hospital gowns. It's the day after Quindlan tried to kill me. All I have to show for it are a few cuts and bruises, but my doctor says I've been through severe psychological trauma, so he kept me overnight for observation. As far as I know, I'm still sane.

"Yeah," Hawk says. "I was the one. Will and I made a deal and he helped me bust up a pretty big drug ring. I never expected we'd become such good friends. But we did."

"It's so weird," I say. "The whole time, I thought you were a dealer."

He smiles sadly and taps his nose bolt. "Yeah, well, my boss has me work in the high schools because of my baby face."

209

Today Hawk's Mohawk is dyed red, blue, yellow, and green—colors of the rainbow—to celebrate with the GLBT community in Austin. The killer is finally off the streets.

"And what about Quindlan?" I say. "Do you know him well?"

"Not really. Quindlan and I worked narcotics together, and we were both close to Will. But I never fully trusted the guy. There was something about him that made my skin crawl. Anyway, the day you showed me Will's book, I started to suspect he was the killer. It was just a hunch. I shared this with a few people in my department, but they thought I was crazy. There was no way to prove it, but I had the date—November tenth. So that morning I followed Quindlan, but he took off in a car and I lost sight of him. That's why I came to school and asked if you knew where he was. When you said no, I found Doomsday on the Drag and he mentioned the warehouse off Manor. He'd been there once with Quindlan. He led me right to the place. So I called my captain and asked for backup."

On my nightstand is a plate of chocolate chip cookies Carson's mom baked for me. I pick it up and offer the cookies to Hawk. He takes three, shoves one into his mouth, and chews. "Hey, these are good." He nabs two more. I offer him the carton of milk left over from lunch. He rips open the top and chugs.

"Hawk? Thanks. Seriously, dude, you saved my life. I'd probably be dead right now if you hadn't shown up at the warehouse."

Hawk wipes his mouth with the back of his hand. "Ah, don't give me too much credit, Noah. I was just doing my job. Plus, you gave Quindlan a pretty good wallop with that fake leg. Totally knocked him out. You may have saved both our sorry butts."

"So, where is he now?" I say.

"As we speak, Quindlan is being transported to the Travis County Jail."

"Where Warren Banks is?"

"Yes. Banks will be released soon. And now that we have Quindlan in custody, and know more about his background, the police will be investigating his involvement in three unsolved murders of teenage boys in the South Bronx—all connected with God's Warriors."

"Whoa. So this isn't his first string of murders."

"Probably not. But it's definitely his last. Oh, I almost forgot." Hawk reaches into his front pocket. He hands me Will's book. "For you, Noah."

"But . . . I don't understand. Don't the police need that for evidence? For the trial?"

"No. Quindlan confessed to all three murders in Austin. We have him stone-cold. So, please, the book is yours. Will would have wanted you to have it."

† † †

Later that afternoon, a reporter from KUT calls my hospital room and asks for a brief interview. He promises it'll be real low key—just him, jotting stuff down and recording our conversation on a mini tape player. My parents aren't exactly thrilled about the idea, but I decide to do it.

"So, Noah, I've heard some interesting rumors about the

weapon you used to subdue the killer until the police arrived. A prosthetic leg? Is this true?"

"Well, yes, it is. You see, my friend's father owns a company, Prosthetics Inc. . . ." I go on to tell the reporter the story, and I sure hope the DPCP is listening.

I find out from the reporter that everyone in Austin thinks I'm this amazing hero, some kind of badass vigilante, which is pretty funny when you think about it. I mean, I fell into Quindlan's trap. Took his bait—hook, line, and sinker. Never suspected he was the enemy, never thought he could be guilty of such heinous crimes. Honestly, the whole thing makes me wonder if there's a hell. Part of me hopes so. But then again, maybe hell is right here on earth. Maybe it's a place inside a person. An evil, wicked place. A choice. It's a scary, sobering thought.

I answer most of the reporter's questions, but I don't speak much about the three victims—Will, Kyle, and Paul. I try not to think about them buried at the cemetery, in Potter's Field. I try not to think about how I was able to escape but they never had a chance.

"So, Noah, as you probably know, the GLBT community in Austin is relieved that the killer has been caught. Considering the nature of these crimes, your religious background, and the fact that you're about the same age as all three victims, I believe both gay and straight people would be interested to hear your opinion regarding homosexuality and the church."

This is not a question I'm prepared for. I take a deep breath. "Well, lately I haven't been a regular churchgoer. And before I met Will, I didn't know any gay people. Not well, anyway. So I didn't think too much about it. But after Kyle's murder and after Will and I got to know each other, things changed. I thought about that issue a lot. I was angry with my family, with the church, for being so judgmental. But pretty soon I realized that I had some prejudices to overcome too. And believe me, that wasn't easy to face. Meeting Will helped me see things more clearly." I glance up at the reporter. He's nodding like he understands.

"Anyway," I go on, "most evangelicals like to say, 'Hate the sin, but love the sinner.' But I don't believe being gay is a sin; it's just part of who a gay person is. The church should reach out to everyone, love and accept people for who they are. At least, that's how I see it."

"And does your father, the Bible Answer Guy, understand your viewpoint?"

"I don't know. There's a chance, in time, he might see things differently. Recently I found out there are some people in our church who are more open-minded. That makes me hopeful."

The reporter nods again. "That's great news. And, Noah, one final question: now that the police have the killer in custody, do you have any plans for the near future?"

I consider this for a moment. My eyes scan the room and land on Will's book. "Yes, I do. My friend Will encouraged me to keep writing music. I have his book of poetry, and I'd like to use his poems as lyrics for my songs. I guess it's just a small thing, but for me it's a start."

That evening I go home. My mom cooks my favorite meal—lamb chops with mashed potatoes—and I watch Nickelodeon with Melanie. My parents are quiet and don't ask too many questions. I'm grateful. Over the next few days, I sleep a lot. The story of Quindlan's arrest is all over the news. I watch some of it, and when it gets to be too much, I turn off the TV. On my third night home, my father knocks on my bedroom door. "Noah, may I come in?"

"Yeah. Sure, Dad."

He walks in and takes a seat beside me on the bed. "I drove out to Memorial Cemetery today. Will's grave looked so bare. I was wondering if there was an inscription you'd like to be placed on his headstone. I'd be happy to do it."

I look at my dad. He's tired. His face is thinner, like he's lost weight. He's reaching out to me, I know, but I'm not sure I'm ready. "Maybe, Dad. Let me think about it, okay?"

"Sure. Just let me know."

† † †

A week later I go back to school, and on the following Saturday afternoon, my father asks me to take a drive with him. He says he has something to show me.

It's a beautiful day. The sky is blue and the leaves on the trees are red, orange, and gold. He parks the car outside Memorial Cemetery. In the distance I see a group of people gathered on the hill near Will's grave. As my dad and I walk across the field, I see Aubrey, Carson, Melanie, and my mom waiting for us. Doomsday and Hawk are coming from the other direction. Marty and a few of the youth group zealots are there too. Even Pastor Simpson. He waves to us.

Melanie walks over to greet me. "Hey, Noah. Are you okay?"

"Yeah, Mel. I think so."

"Good. Come and see." She takes my hand and leads me to Will's grave. A few days ago I told my father what I'd like inscribed on Will's headstone. I read it now.

WILL REED
1993–2010
YOUR WORDS SLICE LIKE A DIAMOND,
A MILLION FACETS OF LIGHT

My father comes up beside me. "Do you like it?"

"Yes, Dad, I do. Thank you."

"Noah, I just want to say that I've made a lot of mistakes in the past. Lately I've begun to see things in a different way. I don't know all the answers, but I do know this: I'll stand behind you. Always. No matter what."

I look at my dad. And then I do something I haven't done in a very long time. I give him a hug.

"Please, everyone, gather around," Pastor Simpson says. To my surprise, he doesn't begin reading from the Bible or ask us to sing a hymn. Instead, he says, "John, will you please say a word for us?"

"Yes," my dad says. We make a circle around Will's grave. He continues. "Thank you all for coming. When Noah brought Will to our house a number of weeks ago, Will told us about his plan to move to California after he graduated. He wanted to work with gay foster kids, help them have a better life. My reaction was not what it should have been. I realize that now."

He pauses and takes a deep breath. "When we found out

Will had been murdered, Noah was devastated. It tore us all apart. I wanted to do something. Something for Will. But I didn't know what. And soon I began to realize that right here in Austin, there are so many foster children who, once they turn eighteen, are forced to leave their homes. Many have no support, nowhere to go. So I looked into some local programs and found one I'd like our church to work with. It's called LifeWorks Austin. In a few weeks, a group of us will be getting some apartments ready for at-risk young people to move into. There are lots of opportunities, like teaching life skills, helping them find jobs, and assisting them with college. It's a small way King of Glory can genuinely help the community."

My dad pauses again and glances around the circle. "Also, after some serious soul-searching, I spoke with Pastor Simpson about the Exodus Group. Our church has decided to discontinue the program."

Across the way, I see Marty smiling. I look at Aubrey; she gives me a quick nod. I know that our church still has a long way to go, and I'm sure there are plenty of battles ahead, but this is a start.

When my dad is finished talking, I notice that Doomsday is about to leave. "Dad? Come here, I want you to meet someone."

We hurry over to Doomsday. "Doomsday, wait." He turns around. I can tell he feels uncomfortable around the crowd of people. "I want you to meet my father."

My dad holds out his hand. Doomsday glances up shyly and shakes it.

"I want to say thank you," my dad says, "for leading the police to Noah. Because of you, he's alive."

Doomsday lowers his eyes. "Oh, well, it's the least I could do. I only wish I could have done more for Will."

"We all feel that way," my dad says. "But thank you. For helping my son."

A dog starts barking. I peer into the distance and see Hercules. He's waiting for Doomsday. "I should go," Doomsday says. "It was so nice to meet you, Dr. Nordstrom. I'm sure Noah's told you how much I enjoy your show."

"Please, call me John," my dad says. "Would you like to come with us, get something to eat?"

"Oh, no, I'm fine, thank you."

"Are you sure?"

"Oh, yes. I'm sure."

"Doomsday? I'll stop by the Drag next weekend," I say. "Maybe you can read me some more Walt Whitman?"

"Yes, I'd like that. And, Noah, I want to tell you something. I know Will kept secrets from me because he thought I wouldn't understand. He thought I would judge him. But I knew. And it didn't matter. Will was a great friend."

"He thought a lot of you," I say.

Doomsday smiles sadly, turns, and walks away. My dad and I stand there, watching helplessly.

Suddenly I hear footsteps behind us. Someone running. I turn and see Hawk. He waves to my dad and me, then yells, "Doomsday! Remember, we were going to have coffee?"

When Hawk reaches Doomsday, he puts an arm around his shoulder. They unleash Hercules from the tree and walk off together into the distance.

"Will he be okay?" my dad asks.

"I don't know. I hope so."

Later that night, I finally take out my guitar and begin to play. I read Will's poems too, even the dark, depressing ones. As I do, I begin to realize that even though there's a lot of evil in the world, there's also a lot of truth and beauty. I think Will knew that best.

† † †

Carson lucks out. On the day of his baptism, it's sixty-five degrees and sunny. Right now, he's waist-deep in Kat's pool, and thanks to our intense weight training, he's looking fairly buff. Marty, the dunker, is beside him, and the two are talking quietly. The youth group is gathered around the patio, and Kat's mom has set out refreshments. Aubrey is sitting on the other end of the pool, watching me. I see the bright yellow straps of her swimsuit—a bikini, I hope—underneath her clothes. I wave. She waves back.

Surprisingly, the DPCP is here. Carson's mom begged him to come, and he gave in at the last minute. He was looking pretty uptight until Kat's mom pulled through and brought him a beer. Evangelicals don't normally serve alcohol at their get-togethers, especially baptisms, so I was pleased she made an exception. He's not exactly smiling, but he doesn't look like he's on the verge of an aneurism either. He sees me and raises a hand in greeting. We've become a lot friendlier, now that he knows I'm not the lead zealot, and now that Prosthetics Inc. has gotten some good press.

Finally Marty begins. "Welcome, everyone. We're here to celebrate with our friend Carson." Marty goes through the usual mumbo jumbo, stuff I've heard a million times—

how baptism is about change, a new birth, a new beginning. But then he says something else. "Jesus also spoke about a baptism of fire. Sometimes it's pain and suffering that causes our rebirth."

I wonder if that's what I've been through. A baptism of fire. It sure feels like it.

Carson's lips are turning blue now. Marty turns to him. "Carson, is there anything you'd like to say?"

"Oh, yeah. Um, thanks, Mom, thanks, Dad, for coming." His teeth are chattering. "Can we do it now?"

"Sure."

When Carson rises out of the water, he's smiling. Kat jumps into the water and gives him a hug. Without even thinking, I whip off my shirt and dive into the pool. The rest of the youth group does the same. I swim underwater, searching for Aubrey. And then I see her, eyes open, heading straight for me.

{author's note}

Like Noah, I grew up in a strict evangelical home. My parents are wonderful people, but as a teen I struggled with the church's legalism, hypocrisy, and exclusivity. I began reading the Bible at a young age, and I never understood how pastors and church members could judge and even condemn others, especially when Jesus was the ultimate example of love and compassion. Ironically, the only people Jesus ever lashed out against were the religious leaders of the time. He called them hypocrites, a brood of vipers who shut the gates to the kingdom of heaven in men's faces. To me that speaks volumes, even today.

As a teenager, I had a few gay friends and acquaintances in the church, but they stayed in the closet. The church taught that homosexuality was a terrible sin, so I imagine they lived with shame, guilt, and fear of going to hell. I wish I had understood more about my gay friends at the time, done something to help them, but it was the 1970s, gays were largely misunderstood, and I had no clue what they were going through.

When I went to college, I lost touch with these people, but I heard about some of their fates. Two of the young men finally came out in their midtwenties, but their churches, friends, and families rejected them. Another young man left home to find a more tolerant community but eventually returned to his family when he was dying of AIDS. I can only hope he passed away with dignity.

Today the future is looking brighter for the GLBT community, but evangelical Christians still hold tightly to their fear and prejudice. Many right-wing Christian conservatives, like Pat Robertson, James Dobson, and the late Jerry Falwell, have publicly denounced gays and lesbians, claiming they have sinful and perverse lifestyles. Other prominent Christian leaders, like Rick Warren and Joel Osteen, who seem to take a more loving approach, still maintain that the Bible teaches that homosexuality is a sin. They claim to welcome gay people, but if you dig a little deeper, you'll find that they also insist that gay Christians need to change their sexual orientation—or remain celibate. I'd like to see how many empty pews there would be in these churches if they told heterosexuals the same thing!

These Christian leaders claim that the Bible says homosexuality is a sin, but . . . does it really? If you've grown up in an evangelical home, you may be surprised by the answer. And if you're a gay teenager burdened by strict evangelical teachings, I hope the truth will set you free from any guilt, fear, or shame you've had to endure.

There are only six references to homosexuality in the

Bible, and Christians who take the time and care to understand them in the light of the Bible's ancient time and culture—after all, it was written thousands of years ago!—will understand what is truly being said.

So here they are. The six "clobber" passages that so many evangelical teachers quote to support their hard stance against homosexuality.

1) Genesis 19—The story of Sodom

Two angels (in the form of men) came to Lot's house in Sodom. The men of the city gathered at Lot's door and demanded that Lot bring these men outside so they could have sex with them. Ultimately, God destroyed Sodom with fire and brimstone. But was the sin of Sodom homosexuality? The answer is no. From archaeological records, we know that it was a common practice in the Near East for men to use homosexual rape to humiliate their enemies. So the story of Sodom is about mob violence, not homosexual desire.

2 & 3) Leviticus 18:22 and 20:13—Do not lie with mankind as with womankind. This is abomination.

This is just one of a long list of rules God gave to the people of Israel while they were wandering in the desert for forty years. However, this rule comes right after the passage that prohibits eating pork or even touching the skin of a dead pig! Contact with a pig is also referred to as an abomination. How many pastors today would condemn a few strips of bacon or a game of football? And here's something else to consider: To understand scripture, you must study its textual and historical context. Leviticus states that this list of rules was given to prevent the Israelites from doing what the Egyptians and Canaanites did, including worshipping Ishtar, the goddess of fertility, by having sex with male temple prostitutes. This practice was believed to give men special powers and guarantee immortality. So it's possible that this scripture referred to pagan religious practices.

4) Romans 1:21–28—Paul's argument about the decline of mankind

This is probably the scripture that evangelicals use most often to condemn homosexuality. In fact, just recently, I was traveling to Houston for a school visit and heard a well-respected pastor of a mega-church in California on the radio quoting this passage from Romans and saying, "Don't let anyone steer you wrong. The apostle Paul tells us clearly that homosexuality is a perversion." But does he? Again, the answer is no—not if you understand this passage in its historical and cultural context. The Romans worshipped Aphrodite, and in her temple, both homosexual and heterosexual orgies with temple prostitutes took place. This is most likely what Paul was referring to. In this passage, his intention was probably to prohibit cultic sexual practices, not same-sex relationships.

5) Jude 7—Going after strange flesh

Evangelical Christians assume that Jude's reference to "going after strange flesh" refers to homosexuality. For straight people, it seems unnatural to be attracted to someone of the same sex. But this isn't what Jude was referring to.

In Genesis, there is an odd passage about angels taking daughters of humans as wives. Hence: strange flesh. This was the final act that brought judgment on the earth in the form of the great flood. Only Noah and his family were spared.

6) 1 Corinthians 6:9–10—A list of sins

The true meaning of this last passage is the most surprising of all. If you read these verses in a modern translation, like the New International Version (NIV), you'll see that it actually states that homosexuals will not inherit the kingdom of God. Unfortunately, Bible translators may have used their own prejudice against gays to fuel this wrong translation. The word they translate as "homosexual" is *arsenokoitai* in the Greek, and it's quite rare. In fact, the translators don't really know its true meaning. It's a combination of two words—those for "bed" and "male." After a careful investigation by scholars into other texts in which this rare word is used, their best guess is that again, Paul's reference is to cultic sexual practices involving male prostitution.

So there you have it. The six clobber passages are not so frightening after all. And while doing research on this topic, I came upon something very interesting. Did you know that Jesus lovingly reached out to a gay man? If you've grown up in the church, you've probably heard the story of Jesus healing the Roman centurion's servant. The story is recorded in Matthew 8:5–13. When Jesus told the centurion that he would come to his house to heal the man, the centurion said there was no reason for Jesus to make the journey; if Jesus would say the word, his servant would be healed. Jesus healed the servant and praised the centurion, marveling at his faith. Now, here's the reason why this story is important. The Greek word used for "servant" in Matthew's account is *pais*, which can also mean "male lover." At other times, Matthew uses the word *duolos* to describe an ordinary servant. Along with this fact, I'd like to add something circumstantial. The Gospels contain many accounts of people asking Jesus to heal themselves or family members, but this is the only example in which someone asks for the healing of a slave. The concern and the desperate actions of the centurion seem to make more sense if the sick man is not only his servant, but also his male partner.

Throughout history, men have often used the Bible or their high positions in the church to justify their own prejudices. When slaves wanted their freedom, Christian slave owners claimed that slavery was an institution approved by God. When women wanted to vote, men used scriptures to claim that women should be subservient to men. When African Americans wanted civil liberties, men like Jerry Falwell, former evangelical pastor and founder of the Moral Majority, worked diligently against Martin Luther King, Jr., and the civil rights movement. Falwell called racial integration "the work of the devil that would destroy our race eventually." In recent years, before his death, Falwell seemingly abandoned his racial bigotry and instead rallied against gays and lesbians. Of course, most evangelicals today are not so hateful and outspoken, but they still hold to the belief that practicing homosexuals have no part in the church or, for that matter, in the kingdom of God. My hope is that these teachers and leaders will one day be enlightened, discover the truth, and embrace all men and women.

Fortunately, gay Christians and their supporters are beginning to speak out. Also, a number of evangelical Christians have recently come out. Mel White, a former ghostwriter for Jerry Falwell, is an example. Ray Boltz, a Christian singer and songwriter who has won two Dove Awards, is another.

If you're a gay teen living in an evangelical home where friends, pastors, and parents don't understand what you're going through, you're not alone. There are organizations and churches that can help. On the next page I've listed Web sites for you to explore and books for you to check out. For now, I'll end with a quote from Martin Luther King, Jr.: "Truth pressed to the earth will rise again!"

For Further Reading

Web sites

Teach Ministries: www.teach-ministries.org
Evangelicals Concerned: www.ecwr.org
www.gaychristian.net
www.gaychurch.org
www.whosoever.org

Bibliography

The Children Are Free: Reexamining the Biblical Evidence on Same-sex Relationships, by Jeff Miner and John Tyler Connoley. Indianapolis: Found Pearl Press, 2008.

Stranger at the Gate: To Be Gay and Christian in America, by Mel White. New York: Simon & Schuster, 1994.

The God Box, by Alex Sanchez. New York: Simon & Schuster Children's Publishing, 2007.

Associated Baptist Press. April 8, 2009. Bob Allen. May 25, 2009. www.abpnews.com/index.php?option=com_content&task=view&id=3989&Itemid=53

Beliefnet. December 17, 2008. Steven Waldman. May 25, 2009. http://blog.beliefnet.com/stevenwaldman/2008/12/rick-warrens-controversial-com.html

Christian Broadcasting Network. May 25, 2009. CBN.com. May 25, 2009. www.cbn.com/spirituallife/BibleStudyand Theology/Discipleship/bible_on_homosexuality.aspx

The Christian Post. May 13, 2008. Lillian Kwon. May 25, 2009. www.christianpost.com/church/Megachurches/2008/05/joel-osteen-maintains-homosexuality-as-sin-13/index.html

Family Research Council. May 15, 2009. Peter Sprigg. May 25, 2009. www.frc.org/get.cfm?i=PV09E03

The Nation. May 16, 2007. Max Blumenthal. May 25, 2009. www.thenation.com/doc/20070528/blumenthal

{acknowledgments}

Thanks to my friends Helen Hemphill, Varian Johnson, Julie Lake, Brian Yansky, and Frances Yansky, for providing valuable feedback on my early drafts; my fellow Delacorte Dames and Dude, Shana Burg, Varian Johnson (the dude is popular), Margo Rabb, and Jennifer Ziegler; my kids, Liz, Dan, Jonny, and Korina, for cheering me on; my agent, Laura Rennert, for her guidance and enthusiasm; and my lovely editor, Françoise Bui, who planted the idea and helped me find the heart of the story. And a special thanks to Ed, my truest pleasure.

{about the author}

April Lurie is a native New Yorker. She is the author of *The Latent Powers of Dylan Fontaine; Brothers, Boyfriends & Other Criminal Minds;* and *Dancing in the Streets of Brooklyn.* She lives near Austin, Texas, with her husband and their four children. Visit her at www.aprillurie.com.